William Shakespeare, Francis Turner Palgrave

Songs and Sonnets by William Shakespeare

William Shakespeare, Francis Turner Palgrave

Songs and Sonnets by William Shakespeare

ISBN/EAN: 9783744767125

Printed in Europe, USA, Canada, Australia, Japan

Cover: Foto ©Andreas Hilbeck / pixelio.de

More available books at **www.hansebooks.com**

SONGS AND SONNETS

BY

WILLIAM SHAKESPEARE

SONGS AND SONNETS

BY

WILLIAM SHAKESPEARE

—ΝΥΝ ΕΓΝΩΝ ΤΟΝ ΕΡΩΤΑ—

EDITED BY

F. T. PALGRAVE

London

MACMILLAN AND CO.

AND NEW YORK

1887

SONGS

πακτίδος ἀδυμελεστέρα·
χρύσω χρυσοτέρα.

REVEILLEZ

H ARK, hark ! the lark at heaven's gate sings,
 And Phoebus 'gins arise,
His steeds to water at those springs
 On chaliced flowers that lies ;
And winking mary-buds begin
 To ope their golden eyes :
With every thing that pretty is,
 My Lady sweet, arise :
  Arise, arise !

II

FANCY

TELL me where is Fancy bred,
   Or in the heart or in the head?
How begot, how nourishéd?
   —Reply, reply.
It is engender'd in the eyes,
With gazing fed; and Fancy dies
In the cradle where it lies.
   Let us all ring Fancy's knell:
   I'll begin it,—Ding, dong, bell:—
     Ding, dong, bell.

III

SILVIA

WHO is Silvia? what is She
  That all our swains commend her?
Holy, fair and wise is she;
 The heaven such grace did lend her
That she might admired be.

Is she kind as she is fair?
 For beauty lives with kindness:
—Love doth to her eyes repair
 To help him of his blindness,
And, being help'd, inhabits there.

Then to Silvia let us sing
 That Silvia is excelling;
She excels each mortal thing
 Upon the dull earth dwelling:
To her let us garlands bring.

IV

YOUTH AND LOVE

O Mistress mine, where are you roaming?
   O stay and hear; your true-love's coming
That can sing both high and low:
Trip no further, pretty sweeting;
Journeys end in lovers meeting,
   Every wise man's son doth know.

What is Love? 'tis not hereafter;
Present mirth hath present laughter;
   What's to come is still unsure:
In delay there lies no plenty;
Then come kiss me, sweet and-twenty :—
   Youth's a stuff will not endure.

V

IT VER ET VENUS

IT was a Lover and his Lass,
    With a hey, and a ho, and a hey nonino,
That o'er the green corn-field did pass
    In the spring time, the only pretty ring time,
When birds do sing, hey ding a ding, ding :
        Sweet lovers love the spring.

Between the acres of the rye
These pretty country folks would lie.

This carol they began that hour,
How that a life was but a flower :

And therefore take the present time,
    With a hey, and a ho, and a hey nonino ;
For love is crownéd with the prime
    In the spring time, the only pretty ring time,
When birds do sing, hey ding a ding, ding :
        Sweet lovers love the spring.

VI

TWO MAIDS WOOING A MAN

Autolycus—Dorcas—Mopsa

A. GET you hence, for I must go
      Where it fits not you to know !
  D. Whither ? *M.* O whither? *D.* Whither?
  M. It becomes thy oath full well
     Thou to me thy secrets tell.
  D. Me, too, let me go thither.
  M. Or thou goest to the grange or mill.
  D. If to either, thou dost ill.
A. Neither. *D.* What, neither ? *A.* Neither.
  D. Thou hast sworn my Love to be.
  M. Thou hast sworn it more to me :
     —Then whither goest ? say, whither ?

VII

RED AND WHITE

IF She be made of white and red,
  Her faults will ne'er be known ;
For blushing cheeks by faults are bred
  And fears by pale white shown :
Then if she fear, or be to blame,
  By this you shall not know,—
For still her cheeks possess the same
  Which native she doth owe !

VIII

LOVE'S DESPAIR

TAKE, O, take those lips away
  That so sweetly were forsworn ;
And those eyes, the break of day,
  Lights that do mislead the morn :
But my kisses bring again ;
Seals of love, but seal'd in vain ;
      —Seal'd in vain.

IX

THE LOVER'S OFFERING

HANG there, my verse, in witness of my love :
　　And thou, thrice-crownéd Queen of night,
　　　survey
With thy chaste eye, from thy pale sphere above,
　　Thy huntress' name that my full life doth sway.
O Rosalind ! these trees shall be my books,
　　And in their barks my thoughts I'll character ;
That every eye which in this forest looks
　　Shall see thy virtue witness'd every where.
Run, run, Orlando ; carve on every tree
The fair, the chaste, and unexpressive She.

X

A SUPPLICATION

SWEET Mistress,—what your name is else, I
    know not,
Nor by what wonder you do hit of mine,—
Less in your knowledge and your grace you show
    not
Than our earth's wonder, more than earth, divine.
Teach me, dear creature, how to think and speak ;
    Lay open to my earthy-gross conceit,
Smother'd in errors, feeble, shallow, weak,
    The folded meaning of your words' deceit.
Against my soul's pure truth why labour you
    To make it wander in an unknown field ?
Are you a god ? would you create me new ?
    Transform me then, and to your power I'll yield !

XI

EROS AND ANTEROS

ART thou, god, to shepherd turn'd,
    That a maiden's heart hath burn'd?
Why, thy godhead laid apart,
Warr'st thou with a woman's heart?
Whiles the eye of man did woo me,
That could do no vengeance to me.
If the scorn of your bright eyne
Hath power to raise such love in mine,
Alack, in me what strange effect
Would they work in mild aspect!
Whiles you chid me, I did love;
How then might your prayers move!
He that brings this love to thee
Little knows this love in me:
And by him seal up thy mind;
Whether that thy youth and kind
Will the faithful offer take
Of me and all that I can make;
Or else by him my love deny,
And then I'll study how to die.

XII

MORNING TEARS

SO sweet a kiss the golden sun gives not
  To those fresh morning drops upon the rose,
As thy eye-beams, when their fresh rays have smote
  The night of dew that on my cheeks down flows:

Nor shines the silver moon one half so bright
  Through the transparent bosom of the deep,
As doth thy face through tears of mine give light;
  Thou shinest in every tear that I do weep:

No drop but as a coach doth carry thee;
  So ridest thou triumphing in my woe.
Do but behold the tears that swell in me,
  And they thy glory through my grief will show:

But do not love thyself; then thou wilt keep
My tears for glasses, and still make me weep.
O Queen of queens! how far dost thou excel,
No thought can think, nor tongue of mortal tell.

XIII

PRAISE OF THE MISTRESS

IF love make me forsworn, how shall I swear to
    love?
  Ah, never faith could hold, if not to beauty
    vow'd!
Though to myself forsworn, to thee I'll faithful
    prove;
  Those thoughts to me were oaks, to thee like
    osiers bow'd.
Study his bias leaves and makes his book thine
    eyes,
  Where all those pleasures live that art would
    comprehend:
If knowledge be the mark, to know thee shall
    suffice;

Well learnéd is that tongue that well can thee
    commend,
All ignorant that soul that sees thee without
    wonder ;
  Which is to me some praise that I thy parts
    admire ·
Thy eye Jove's lightning bears, thy voice his
    dreadful thunder,
  Which, not to anger bent, is music and sweet
    fire.
Celestial as thou art, O pardon, Love, this wrong,
That sings heaven's praise with such an earthly
    tongue !

XIV

LOVE THE ONLY STUDENT

STUDY me how to please the eye indeed
    By fixing it upon a fairer eye,
Who dazzling so, that eye shall be his heed,
    And give him light that it was blinded by.

Study is like the heaven's glorious sun
    That will not be deep-search'd with saucy looks :
Small have continual plodders ever won
    Save base authority from others' books.

These earthly godfathers of heaven's lights
    That give a name to every fixéd star,
Have no more profit of their shining nights
    Than those that walk and wot not what they are.

Too much to know is to know nought but fame,
And every godfather can give a name.

XV

THE PERJURIES OF LOVE

DID not the heavenly rhetoric of thine eye,
  'Gainst whom the world cannot hold argument,
Persuade my heart to this false perjury?
  Vows for thee broke deserve not punishment.

A woman I forswore; but I will prove,
  Thou being a goddess, I forswore not thee.
My vow was earthly, thou a heavenly love;
  Thy grace being gain'd cures all disgrace in me.

Vows are but breath, and breath a vapour is:
  Then thou, fair Sun, which on my earth dost
    shine,
Exhalest this vapour-vow; in thee it is:
  If broken, then, it is no fault of mine:

If by me broke, what fool is not so wise
To lose an oath, to win a paradise?

XVI

THE LONGING THAT CANNOT BE UTTERED

ON a day—alack the day !—
       Love, whose month is ever May,
Spied a blossom passing fair
Playing in the wanton air :
Through the velvet leaves the wind,
All unseen, can passage find ;
That the Lover, sick to death,
Wish himself the heaven's breath.
—Air, quoth he, thy cheeks may blow ;
Air, would I might triumph so !
But, alack, my hand is sworn
Ne'er to pluck thee from thy thorn ;
Vow, alack, for youth unmeet,
Youth so apt to pluck a sweet !
Do not call it sin in me,
That I am forsworn for thee ;
Thou,—for whom Jove would swear
Juno but an Ethiope were,
And deny himself for Jove,
Turning mortal for thy love.

XVII

EPITHALAMIUM

THEN is there mirth in Heaven,
   When earthly things made even
  Atone together !
Good duke, receive thy daughter :
Hymen from heaven brought her,
   Yea, brought her hither,
That thou mightest join her hand with his
Whose heart within his bosom is.

SONG

Wedding is great Juno's crown :
  O blessèd bond of board and bed !
'Tis Hymen peoples every town ;
  High Wedlock then be honourèd :
Honour, high honour and renown,
To Hymen, god of every town !

XVIII

SONG OF BLESSING

HONOUR, riches, marriage-blessing,
    Long continuance, and increasing,
Hourly joys be still upon you !
Juno sings her blessings on you.

Earth's increase, foison plenty,
Barns and garners never empty
Vines with clustering bunches growing,
Plants with goodly burthen bowing ;

Spring come to you at the farthest
In the very end of harvest !
Scarcity and want shall shun you ;
Ceres' blessing so is on you.

XIX

MAN AND WOMAN

SIGH no more, ladies, sigh no more,—
   Men were deceivers ever,
One foot in sea and one on shore,
   To one thing constant never :
—Then sigh not so, but let them go,
   And be you blithe and bonny,
Converting all your sounds of woe
   Into, Hey nonny, nonny.

Sing no more ditties, sing no more,
   Of dumps so dull and heavy ;
The fraud of men was ever so
   Since summer first was leafy :
—Then sigh not so, but let them go,
   And be you blithe and bonny,
Converting all your sounds of woe
   Into, Hey nonny, nonny.

XX

THE YOUTH'S DIRGE

COME away, come away, Death,
　　And in sad cypres let me be laid ;
Fly away, fly away, breath ;
　I am slain by a fair cruel maid.
My shroud of white, stuck all with yew,
　　O, prepare it !
My part of death, no one so true
　　Did share it.

Not a flower, not a flower sweet,
　On my black coffin let there be strown ;
Not a friend, not a friend greet
　My poor corpse, where my bones shall be
　　　thrown :
A thousand thousand sighs to save,
　　Lay me, O, where
Sad true lover never find my grave,
　　To weep there.

XXI

DIRGES

SWEET Flower, with flowers thy bridal bed I
    strew,—
  O woe ! thy canopy is dust and stones ;—
Which with sweet water nightly I will dew,
  Or, wanting that, with tears distilled by moans :
The obsequies that I for thee will keep
Nightly shall be to strew thy grave and weep.

    Pardon, Goddess of the night,
    Those that slew thy virgin knight ;
    For the which, with songs of woe,
    Round about her tomb they go.
      Midnight, assist our moan ;
      Help us to sigh and groan,
        Heavily, heavily :
      Graves, yawn and yield your dead
      Till death be utteréd,
        Heavily, heavily.

XXII

THE END

FEAR no more the heat o' the sun
 Nor the furious winter's rages;
Thou thy worldly task hast done,
 Home art gone, and ta'en thy wages:
Golden lads and girls all must,
As chimney-sweepers, come to dust.

Fear no more the frown o' the great;
 Thou art past the tyrant's stroke;
Care no more to clothe and eat;
 To thee the reed is as the oak:
The sceptre, learning, physic, must
All follow this, and come to dust.

Fear no more the lightning-flash
  Nor the all-dreaded thunder-stone ;
Fear not slander, censure rash ;
  Thou hast finish'd joy and moan :
All lovers young, all lovers must
Consign to thee, and come to dust.

    No exorciser harm thee !
    Nor no witchcraft charm thee !
    Ghost unlaid forbear thee !
    Nothing ill come near thee !
    Quiet consummation have ;
    And renownéd be thy grave !

XXIII

THE FAIRY LIFE

I

WHERE the bee sucks, there suck I :
　　In a cowslip's bell I lie ;
There I couch when owls do cry.
On the bat's back I do fly
After summer merrily.
Merrily, merrily shall I live now,
　　Under the blossom that hangs on the bough.

II

Come unto these yellow sands,
   And then take hands :
Courtsied when you have and kiss'd
   The wild waves whist,
Foot it featly here and there ;
And, sweet Sprites, the burthen bear :
   Hark, hark !
      Bow-wow.
   The watch-dogs bark :
      Bow-wow.
   Hark, hark ! I hear
The strain of strutting chanticleer
   Cry, Cock-a-diddle-dow.

III

Over hill, over dale
    Thorough bush, thorough brier
Over park, over pale
    Thorough flood, thorough fire
I do wander every where,
Swifter than the moon's sphere ;
And I serve the fairy Queen,
To dew her orbs upon the green.
The cowslips tall her pensioners be :
In their gold coats spots you see,
Those be rubies, fairy favours,
In those freckles live their savours :
I must go seek some dewdrops here
And hang a pearl in every cowslip's ear.

XXIV

LULLABY

YOU spotted snakes with double tongue,
  Thorny hedgehogs, bè not seen ;
Newts and blind-worms, do no wrong,
  Come not near our fairy Queen !

Weaving spiders, come not here ;
  Hence, you long-legg'd spinners, hence !
Beetles black, approach not near ;
  Worm nor snail, do no offence.

  Philomel, with melody
  Sing in our sweet lullaby ;
Lulla, lulla, lullaby, Lulla, lulla, lullaby :
    Never harm
    Nor spell nor charm
  Come our lovely lady nigh :
  So, Good Night, with lullaby.

XXV
.

THE FAIRY BLESSING

NOW the hungry lion roars
    And the wolf behowls the moon,
Whilst the heavy ploughman snores,
  All with weary task fordone.
Now the wasted brands do glow,
    Whilst the screech-owl, screeching loud,
Puts the wretch that lies in woe
    In remembrance of a shroud.
Now it is the time of night
    That the graves all gaping wide,
Every one lets forth his sprite
    In the church-way paths to glide :
And we Fairies, that do run
    By the triple Hecate's team
From the presence of the sun,
    Following darkness like a dream,
Now are frolic : not a mouse
Shall disturb this hallow'd house :

I am sent with broom before,
To sweep the dust behind the door.

Through the house give glimmering light,
  By the dead and drowsy fire :
Every elf and fairy sprite
  Hop as light as bird from brier ;
And this ditty, after me,
Sing, and dance it trippingly.

First, rehearse your song by rote,
To each word a warbling note :
Hand in hand, with fairy grace,
Will we sing, and bless this place.

Now, until the break of day,
Through this house each fairy stray.
To the best bride-bed will we,
Which by us shall blessèd be ;

And the issue there create
Ever shall be fortunate !
So shall all the couples three
Ever true in loving be ;
And the blots of Nature's hand
Shall not in their issue stand ;
Never mole, hare-lip, nor scar,
Nor mark prodigious, such as are
Despiséd in nativity,
Shall upon their children be.
With this field-dew consecrate,
Every fairy take his gait :
And each several chamber bless,
Through this palace, with sweet peace ;
And the owner of it blest
Ever shall in safety rest.

Trip away ; make no stay ;
Meet me all by break of day.

XXVI

A SINNER TORMENTED

F IE on sinful fantasy !
　Fie on lust and luxury !
Lust is but a bloody fire
Kindled with unchaste desire,
Fed in heart, whose flames aspire
As thoughts do blow them, higher and higher.
Pinch him, fairies, mutually ;
Pinch him for his villany ;
Pinch him, and burn him, and turn him about,
Till candles and starlight and moonshine be out

XXVII

THE WISDOM OF THE FOOL

FATHERS that wear rags
        Do make their children blind;
But fathers that bear bags
    Shall see their children kind.
Fortune, that arrant whore,
Ne'er turns the key to the poor.

That, Sir, which serves and seeks for gain
        And follows but for form,
Will pack when it begins to rain,
    And leave thee in the storm.
But I will tarry; the fool will stay,
    And let the wise man fly;
The knave turns fool that runs away;
    The fool no knave, perdy.

XXVIII

THE PEDLAR'S SONG

WHEN daffodils begin to peer,
    With heigh ! the doxy over the dale,
Why then comes in the sweet o' the year ;
    For the red blood reigns in the winter's pale.

The white sheet bleaching on the hedge,
    With heigh ! the sweet birds, O, how they
        sing !
Doth set my pugging tooth on edge ;
    For a quart of ale is a dish for a king.

The lark, that tirra-lyra chants,
    With heigh ! with heigh ! the thrush and
        the jay,
Are summer songs for me and my aunts,
    While we lie tumbling in the hay.

D

But shall I go mourn for that, my dear?
   The pale moon shines by night:
And when I wander here and there,
   I then do most go right.

If tinkers may have leave to live
   And bear the sow-skin budget,
Then my account I well may give
   And in the stocks avouch it.

Jog on, jog on, the foot-path way,
   And merrily hent the stile-a:
A merry heart goes all the day,
   Your sad, tires in a mile-a.

XXIX

PEDLAR'S CRIES

L AWN as white as driven snow ;
　　Cypress black as e'er was crow ;
Gloves as sweet as damask roses ;
Masks for faces and for noses ;
Bugle bracelet, necklace amber,
Perfume for a lady's chamber ;
Golden quoifs and stomachers,
For my lads to give their dears :
Pins and poking-sticks of steel,
What maids lack from head to heel :
Come buy of me, come ; come buy, come buy ;
　　Buy, lads, or else your lasses cry :
　　　　Come buy.

Will you buy any tape,
Or lace for your cape,
My dainty duck, my dear-a ?
Any silk, any thread,
Any toys for your head,
Of the new'st and finest, finest wear-a ?
Come to the pedlar ;
Money's a medler
That doth utter all men's ware-a.

XXX

BACCHANALIAN SONG

COME, thou Monarch of the vine,
Plumpy Bacchus with pink eyne !
In thy fats our cares be drown'd,
With thy grapes our hairs be crown'd :
Cup us, till the world go round,
Cup us, till the world go round !

XXXI

A COUNTRY FELLOW'S SONG

DO nothing but eat, and make good cheer,
　　And praise God for the merry year ;
When flesh is cheap and females dear,
And lusty lads roam here and there
　　　　So merrily,
And ever among so merrily.

Be merry, be merry, my wife has all ;
For women are shrews, both short and tall :
'Tis merry in hall when beards wag all,
　　And welcome merry Shrove-tide :—
　　　　Be merry, be merry !

A cup of wine that's brisk and fine,
And drink unto the leman mine ;
　　And a merry heart lives long-a.
Fill the cup, and let it come ;
I'll pledge you a mile to the bottom.

XXXII

A CLOWN'S HELEN

WAS this fair face the cause, quoth she,
　　Why the Grecians sackéd Troy ?
Fond done, done fond,
　　Was this King Priam's joy?

With that she sighéd as she stood,
With that she sighéd as she stood,
　　And gave this sentence then ;
Among nine bad if one be good,
Among nine bad if one be good,
　　There's yet one good in ten.

XXXIII

A CLOWN'S SONG

WHEN that I was and a little tiny boy,
  With hey, ho, the wind and the rain,
A foolish thing was but a toy,
  For the rain it raineth every day.

But when I came to man's estate,
'Gainst knaves and thieves men shut their gate.

But when I came, alas ! to wive,
By swaggering could I never thrive.

But when I came unto my beds,
With toss-pots still had drunken heads.

A great while ago the world begun,
  With hey, ho, the wind and the rain,
But that's all one, our play is done,
  And we'll strive to please you every day.

XXXIV

FORESTER'S SONG

WHAT shall he have that kill'd the deer?
His leather skin and horns to wear.
Then sing him home;
Take thou no scorn to wear the horn;
It was a crest ere thou wast born:
Thy father's father wore it,
And thy father bore it!
The horn, the horn, the lusty horn
Is not a thing to laugh to scorn.

XXXV

A SAILOR'S SONG

THE master, the swabber, the boatswain and I,
    The gunner and his mate,
Loved Mall, Meg and Marian and Margery,
    But none of us cared for Kate ;
    For she had a tongue with a tang,
    Would cry to a sailor, Go hang !
She loved not the savour of tar nor of pitch,
Yet a tailor might scratch her where'er she did
    itch :
    Then to sea, boys, and let her go hang !

XXXVI

THE POWER OF SONG

ORPHEUS with his lute made trees
        And the mountain tops that freeze
    Bow themselves when he did sing :
To his music plants and flowers
Ever sprung ; as sun and showers
    There had made a lasting spring.

Every thing that heard him play,
Even the billows of the sea,
    Hung their heads, and then lay by.
In sweet music in such art,
Killing care and grief of heart
    Fall asleep, or hearing, die.

XXXVII

SPRING

WHEN daisies pied and violets blue
      And lady-smocks all silver-white
And cuckoo-buds of yellow hue
   Do paint the meadows with delight,
The cuckoo then, on every tree,
Mocks married men; for thus sings he,
            Cuckoo;
Cuckoo, cuckoo :—O word of fear,
Unpleasing to a married ear !

When shepherds pipe on oaten straws
   And merry larks are ploughmen's clocks,
When turtles tread, and rooks, and daws,
   And maidens bleach their summer smocks,
The cuckoo then, on every tree,
Mocks married men; for thus sings he,
            Cuckoo;
Cuckoo, cuckoo :—O word of fear,
Unpleasing to a married ear !

XXXVIII

WINTER

WHEN icicles hang by the wall
    And Dick the shepherd blows his nail
And Tom bears logs into the hall
   And milk comes frozen home in pail,
When blood is nipp'd and ways be foul,
Then nightly sings the staring owl,
      Tu-whit ;
Tu-who ;—a merry note ;—
While greasy Joan doth keel the pot.

When all aloud the wind doth blow
   And coughing drowns the parson's saw
And birds sit brooding in the snow
   And Marian's nose looks red and raw,
When roasted crabs hiss in the bowl,
Then nightly sings the staring owl,
      Tu-whit ;
Tu-who ;—a merry note ;—
While greasy Joan doth keel the pot.

XXXIX

VENERI VICTRICI

L OVE, Love, nothing but Love, still more !
  For, O, love's bow
  Shoots buck and doe :
  The shaft confounds,
  Not that it wounds,
But tickles still the sore.

These lovers cry Oh ! oh ! they die !
  Yet that which seems the wound to kill,
Doth turn oh ! oh ! to ha ! ha ! he !
  So dying love lives still :
Oh ! oh ! a while, but ha ! ha ! ha !
Oh ! oh ! groans out for ha ! ha ! ha !
                    —Heigh-ho !

XI.

A SEA DIRGE

FULL fathom five thy father lies ;
　　Of his bones are coral made ;
Those are pearls that were his eyes :
　　Nothing of him that doth fade
But doth suffer a sea-change
Into something rich and strange.
Sea-nymphs hourly ring his knell :
　　　Ding-dong.
Hark ! now I hear them,—Ding-dong, bell.

XLI

THE LOST LOVE

HOW should I your true-Love know
    From another one?
By his cockle hat and staff,
    And his sandal shoon.

He is dead and gone, lady,
    He is dead and gone;
At his head a grass-green turf,
    At his heels a stone.

White his shroud as the mountain snow,
    Larded with sweet flowers;—
Which bewept to the grave did go
    With true-love showers.

XLII

SNATCHES

I

THEY bore him barefaced on the bier;
　　Hey non nonny, nonny, hey nonny;
And in his grave rain'd many a tear :—
　　You must sing a-down a-down,
　　An you call him a-down-a.

And will he not come again?
And will he not come again?
　　No, no, he is dead:
　　Go to thy death-bed:
He never will come again.

His beard was as white as snow,
All flaxen was his poll :
  He is gone, he is gone,
  And we cast away moan :
God ha' mercy on his soul !

II

Come o'er the bourn, Bessy, to me !
  —Her boat hath a leak,
  And she must not speak
Why she dares not come over to thee !

III

Sleepest or wakest thou, jolly shepherd?
  Thy sheep be in the corn ;
And for one blast of thy minikin mouth,
  Thy sheep shall take no harm.

.

XLIII

THE MISANTHROPE

IMMORTAL gods, I crave no pelf ;
I pray for no man but myself :
Grant I may never prove so fond,
To trust man on his oath or bond ;
Or a harlot, for her weeping ;
Or a dog, that seems a-sleeping ;
Or a keeper with my freedom ;
Or my friends, if I should need 'em.
Amen.   So fall to't :
Rich men sin, and I eat root.

XLIV

NATURE AND MAN

B LOW, blow, thou winter wind,
  Thou art not so unkind
As man's ingratitude ;
Thy tooth is not so keen,
Because thou art not seen,
  Although thy breath be rude.
Heigh-ho ! sing, heigh-ho ! unto the green holly :
Most friendship is feigning, most loving mere folly :
  Then, heigh-ho, the holly !
  This life is most jolly.

Freeze, freeze, thou bitter sky,
That dost not bite so nigh
   As benefits forgot :
Though thou the waters warp,
Thy sting is not so sharp
   As friend remember'd not.
Heigh-ho ! sing, heigh-ho ! unto the green holly :
Most friendship is feigning, most loving mere folly:
   Then, heigh-ho, the holly !
   This life is most jolly.

XLV

THE WORLD'S WAY

WHY, let the stricken deer go weep,
    The hart ungalléd play ;
For some must watch, while some must sleep :
    So runs the world away.

XLVI

THE LIFE ACCORDING TO NATURE

UNDER the greenwood tree
        Who loves to lie with me,
And turn his merry note
Unto the sweet bird's throat,
Come hither, come hither, come hither !
        Here shall he see
        No enemy
But winter and rough weather.

Who doth ambition shun
And loves to live i' the sun,
Seeking the food he eats
And pleased with what he gets,
Come hither, come hither, come hither :
        Here shall he see
        No enemy
But winter and rough weather.

SONNETS

Ὦ θεοὶ, τίς ἄρα Κύπρις, ἢ τίς Ἵμερος
τοῦδε ξυνήψατο;

TO THE ONLIE BEGETTER OF

THESE INSUING SONNETS

MR. W. H. ALL HAPPINESSE

AND THAT ETERNITIE

PROMISED BY

OUR EVER-LIVING POET

WISHETH

THE WELL-WISHING

ADVENTURER IN

SETTING

FORTH

T. T.

TO HIS FRIEND, THAT HE SHOULD MARRY

FROM fairest creatures we desire increase,
    That thereby beauty's rose might never die,
But as the riper should by time decease,
His tender heir might bear his memory :

But thou, contracted to thine own bright eyes,
Feed'st thy light's flame with self-substantial fuel,
Making a famine where abundance lies,
Thyself thy foe, to thy sweet self too cruel.

Thou that art now the world's fresh ornament
And only herald to the gaudy spring,
Within thine own blood buriest thy content
And, tender churl, mak'st waste in niggarding.

    Pity the world, or else this glutton be,
    To eat the world's due, by the grave and thee.

A REVIVAL

WHEN forty winters shall besiege thy brow,
And dig deep trenches in thy beauty's field,
Thy youth's proud livery, so gazed on now,
Will be a tatter'd weed, of small worth held:

Then being ask'd where all thy beauty lies,
Where all the treasure of thy lusty days,
To say, within thine own deep sunken eyes,
Were an all-eating shame and thriftless praise.

How much more praise deserved thy beauty's use,
If thou couldst answer ' This fair child of mine
Shall sum my count and make my old excuse,'
Proving his beauty by succession thine !

This were to be new made when thou art old,
And see thy blood warm when thou feel'st it cold,

LIFE CONTINUED

LOOK in thy glass, and tell the face thou
    viewest
Now is the time that face should form another;
Whose fresh repair if now thou not renewest,
Thou dost beguile the world, unbless some mother.

For where is she so fair whose unear'd womb
Disdains the tillage of thy husbandry?
Or who is he so fond will be the tomb
Of his self-love, to stop posterity?

Thou art thy mother's glass, and she in thee
Calls back the lovely April of her prime:
So thou through windows of thine age shalt see
Despite of wrinkles this thy golden time.

  But if thou live, remember'd not to be,
  Die single, and thine image dies with thee.

CHILDLESSNESS

UNTHRIFTY loveliness, why dost thou spend
　　Upon thyself thy beauty's legacy?
Nature's bequest gives nothing, but doth lend,
And being frank she lends to those are free.

Then, beauteous niggard, why dost thou abuse
The bounteous largess given thee to give!
Profitless usurer, why dost thou use
So great a sum of sums, yet canst not live?

For having traffic with thyself alone,
Thou of thyself thy sweet self dost deceive.
Then how, when nature calls thee to begone,
What acceptable audit canst thou leave?

　　Thy unused beauty must be tomb'd with thee,
　　Which, uséd, lives th' executor to be.

CHANGE AND CONTINUANCE

THOSE hours, that with gentle work did frame
　　The lovely gaze where every eye doth dwell,
Will play the tyrants to the very same
And that unfair which fairly doth excel ;

For never-resting time leads summer on
To hideous winter and confounds him there ;
Sap check'd with frost and lusty leaves quite gone,
Beauty o'ersnow'd and bareness every where :

Then, were not summer's distillation left,
.A liquid prisoner pent in walls of glass,
Beauty's effect with beauty were bereft,
Nor it nor no remembrance what it was :

　　But flowers distill'd, though they with winter
　　　　meet,
　　Leese but their show ; their substance still lives
　　　　sweet.

PERPETUATION

THEN let not winter's ragged hand deface
   In thee thy summer, ere thou be distill'd :
Make sweet some vial; treasure thou some place
With beauty's treasure, ere it be self-kill'd.

That use is not forbidden usury
Which happies those that pay the willing loan ;
That's for thyself to breed another thee,
Or ten times happier, be it ten for one ;

Ten times thyself were happier than thou art,
If ten of thine ten times refigured thee :
Then what could death do, if thou shouldst depart,
Leaving thee living in posterity ?

  Be not self-will'd, for thou art much too fair
    To be death's conquest and make worms thine
      heir.

FROM SUNRISE TO SUNSET

L O ! in the orient when the gracious light
    Lifts up his burning head, each under eye
Doth homage to his new-appearing sight,
Serving with looks his sacred majesty ;

And having climb'd the steep-up heavenly hill,
Resembling strong youth in his middle age,
Yet mortal looks adore his beauty still,
Attending on his golden pilgrimage ;

But when from highmost pitch, with weary car,
Like feeble age, he reeleth from the day,
The eyes, 'fore duteous, now converted are
From his low tract and look another way :

So thou, thyself out-going in thy noon,
Unlook'd on diest, unless thou get a son.

HARMONY AND MELODY

MUSIC to hear, why hear'st thou music sadly ?
　　Sweets with sweets war not, joy delights in
　　　joy.
Why lov'st thou that which thou receiv'st not
　gladly,
Or else receiv'st with pleasure thine annoy ?

If the true concord of well-tunéd sounds,
By unions married, do offend thine ear,
They do but sweetly chide thee, who confounds
In singleness the parts that thou shouldst bear.

Mark how one string, sweet husband to another,
Strikes each in each by mutual ordering,
Resembling sire and child and happy mother
Who all in one, one pleasing note do sing :

　Whose speechless song, being many, seeming one,
　Sings this to thee : 'thou single wilt prove none.'

A WARNING

IS it for fear to wet a widow's eye '
    That thou consum'st thyself in single life?
Ah ! if thou issueless shalt hap to die,
The world will wail thee, like a makeless wife ;

The world will be thy widow and still weep
That thou no form of thee hast left behind,
When every private widow well may keep
By children's eyes her husband's shape in mind.

Look, what an unthrift in the world doth spend
Shifts but his place, for still the world enjoys it ;
But beauty's waste hath in the world an end,
And kept unused, the user so destroys it.

    No love toward others in that bosom sits
    That on himself such murderous shame commits.

F

AN APPEAL

FOR shame! deny that thou bear'st love to any,
　　Who for thyself art so unprovident.
Grant, if thou wilt, thou art beloved of many,
But that thou none lov'st is most evident;

For thou art so possess'd with murderous hate
That 'gainst thyself thou stick'st not to conspire,
Seeking that beauteous roof to ruinate
Which to repair should be thy chief desire.

O, change thy thought, that I may change my mind!
Shall hate be fairer lodged than gentle love?
Be, as thy presence is, gracious and kind,
Or to thyself at least kind-hearted prove:

　　Make thee another self for love of me,
　　That beauty still may live in thine or thee.

A MAN'S DUTY

A S fast as thou shalt wane, so fast thou growest
   In one of thine, from that which thou departest;
And that fresh blood which youngly thou bestowest
Thou mayst call thine when thou from youth con-
      vertest.

Herein lives wisdom, beauty, and increase;
Without this, folly, age, and cold decay :
If all were minded so, the times should cease
And threescore year would make the world away.

Let those whom Nature hath not made for store,
Harsh, featureless, and rude, barrenly perish :
Look, whom she best endow'd she gave the more ;
Which bounteous gift thou shouldst in bounty
      cherish :

She carved thee for her seal, and meant thereby
Thou shouldst print more, not let that copy die.

ALL THINGS FADE

WHEN I do count the clock that tells the time,
　　And see the brave day sunk in hideous night;
When I behold the violet past prime,
And sable curls all silver'd o'er with white;

When lofty trees I see barren of leaves
Which erst from heat did canopy the herd,
And summer's green all girded up in sheaves
Borne on the bier with white and bristly beard,

Then of thy beauty do I question make,
That thou among the wastes of time must go,
Since sweets and beauties do themselves forsake
And die as fast as they see others grow;

　　And nothing 'gainst Time's scythe can make
　　　　defence
　　Save breed, to brave him when he takes thee
　　　　hence.

PRESENT AND FUTURE

O, THAT you were yourself ! but, Love, you are
 No longer yours than you yourself here live:
Against this coming end you should prepare,
And your sweet semblance to some other give.

So should that beauty which you hold in lease
 Find no determination ; then you were
Yourself again after yourself's decease,
 When your sweet issue your sweet form should bear.

Who lets so fair a house fall to decay,
Which husbandry in honour might uphold
Against the stormy gusts of winter's day
And barren rage of death's eternal cold ?

 O, none but unthrifts ! Dear my Love, you know
 You had a father : let your son say so.

THE PROPHECIES OF LOVE

NOT from the stars do I my judgement pluck ;
　　And yet methinks I have astronomy,
But not to tell of good or evil luck,
Of plagues, of dearths, or seasons' quality ;

Nor can I fortune to brief minutes tell,
Pointing to each his thunder, rain and wind,
Or say with princes if it shall go well,
By oft predict that I in heaven find :

But from thine eyes my knowledge I derive,
And, constant stars, in them I read such art
As truth and beauty shall together thrive,
If from thyself to store thou wouldst convert ;

　Or else of thee this I prognosticate :
　Thy end is truth's and beauty's doom and date.

YOUTH AND TIME

WHEN I consider everything that grows
    Holds in perfection but a little moment,
That this huge stage presenteth nought but shows
Whereon the stars in secret influence comment;

When I perceive that men as plants increase,
Cheer'd and check'd even by the self-same sky,
Vaunt in their youthful sap, at height decrease
And wear their brave state out of memory;

Then the conceit of this inconstant stay
Sets you most rich in youth before my sight,
Where wasteful Time debateth with Decay
To change your day of youth to sullied night;

   And all in war with Time for love of you,
   As he takes from you, I engraft you new.

COUNSELS OF LOVE

BUT wherefore do not you a mightier way
    Make war upon this bloody tyrant, Time?
And fortify yourself in your decay
With means more blesséd than my barren rhyme?

Now stand you on the top of happy hours,
And many maiden gardens yet unset
With virtuous wish would bear your living flowers,
Much liker than your painted counterfeit :

So should the lines of life that life repair,
Which this, Time's pencil, or my pupil pen,
Neither in inward worth nor outward fair,
Can make you live yourself in eyes of men.

    To give away yourself keeps yourself still,
    And you must live, drawn by your own sweet skill.

LOVE AS PAINTER

WHO will believe my verse in time to come,
  If it were fill'd with your most high deserts?
Though yet, heaven knows, it is but as a tomb
Which hides your life and shows not half your parts.

If I could write the beauty of your eyes
And in fresh numbers number all your graces,
The age to come would say 'This poet lies ;
Such heavenly touches ne'er touch'd earthly faces.'

So should my papers yellow'd with their age
Be scorn'd like old men of less truth than tongue,
And your true rights be term'd a poet's rage
And stretchéd metre of an antique song :

  But were some child of yours alive that time,
  You should live twice ; in it and in my rhyme.

THE UNFADING PICTURE

SHALL I compare thee to a summer's day?
  Thou art more lovely and more temperate :
Rough winds do shake the darling buds of May
And summer's lease hath all too short a date :

Sometime too hot the eye of heaven shines,
And often is his gold complexion dimm'd ;
And every fair from fair sometime declines,
By chance or nature's changing course untrimm'd ;

But thy eternal summer shall not fade
Nor lose possession of that fair thou owest ;
Nor shall Death brag thou wander'st in his shade
When in eternal lines to time thou growest :

  So long as men can breathe or eyes can see,
  So long lives this ;—and this gives life to thee.

THAT TIME SHOULD SPARE
HIS FRIEND

DEVOURING Time, blunt thou the lion's paws,
      And make the earth devour her own sweet
            brood ;
Pluck the keen teeth from the fierce tiger's jaws,
And burn the long-lived phoenix in her blood ;

Make glad and sorry seasons as thou fleets,
And do whate'er thou wilt, swift-footed Time,
To the wide world and all her fading sweets ;
But I forbid thee one most heinous crime :

O, carve not with thy hours my Love's fair brow
Nor draw no lines there with thine antique pen ;
Him in thy course untainted do allow
For beauty's pattern to succeeding men.

   Yet, do thy worst, old Time : despite thy wrong,
   My Love shall in my verse ever live young.

FOR PRAISE NOT COMPLIMENT

SO is it not with me as with that Muse
　　Stirr'd by a painted beauty to his verse,
Who heaven itself for ornament doth use
And every fair with his fair doth rehearse;

Making a couplement of proud compare
With sun and moon, with earth and sea's rich gems,
With April's first-born flowers, and all things rare
That heaven's air in this huge rondure hems.

O, let me, true in love, but truly write,
And then believe me, my Love is as fair
As any mother's child, though not so bright
As those gold candles fix'd in heaven's air:

　　Let them say more that like of hearsay well;
　　I will not praise that purpose not to sell.

LOVE EQUALIZES HEARTS

MY glass shall not persuade me I am old,
　　So long as youth and thou are of one date ;
But when in thee time's furrows I behold
Then look I death my days should expiate.

For all that beauty that doth cover thee
Is but the seemly raiment of my heart,
Which in thy breast doth live, as thine in me ;
How can I then be elder than thou art ?

O, therefore, Love, be of thyself so wary
As I, not for myself, but for thee will ;
Bearing thy heart, which I will keep so chary
As tender nurse her babe from faring ill.

　Presume not on thy heart when mine is slain ;
　Thou gav'st me thine, not to give back again.

LOVE'S SPEECH AND SILENCE

As an unperfect actor on the stage
　　Who with his fear is put besides his part,
Or some fierce thing replete with too much rage,
Whose strength's abundance weakens his own
　　heart,

So I, for fear of trust, forget to say
The perfect ceremony of love's rite,
And in mine own love's strength seem to decay,
O'ercharged with burden of mine own love's might.

O, let my books be then the eloquence
And dumb presagers of my speaking breast,
Who plead for love and look for recompense
More than that tongue that more hath more
　　express'd.

　　O, learn to read what silent love hath writ :
　　To hear with eyes belongs to love's fine wit.

THE PICTURE

MINE eye hath play'd the painter, and hath
    stell'd
Thy beauty's form in table of my heart ;
My body is the frame wherein 'tis held,
And pérspective it is best painter's art.

For through the painter must you see his skill,
To find where your true image pictured lies ;
Which in my bosom's shop is hanging still,
That hath his windows glazéd with thine eyes.

Now see what good turns eyes for eyes have done :
Mine eyes have drawn thy shape, and thine for me
Are windows to my breast, where-through the sun
Delights to peep, to gaze therein on thee ;

    Yet eyes this cunning want to grace their art ;
    They draw but what they see, know not the
        heart.

A BOAST

LET those who are in favour with their stars
    Of public honour and proud titles boast,
Whilst I, whom fortune of such triumph bars,
Unlook'd for joy in that I honour most.

Great princes' favourites their fair leaves spread
But as the marigold at the sun's eye,
And in themselves their pride lies buriéd,
For at a frown they in their glory die.

The painful warrior famouséd for fight,
After a thousand victories once foil'd,
Is from the book of honour razéd quite,
And all the rest forgot for which he toil'd:

    Then happy I, that love and am beloved
    Where I may not remove, nor be removed.

L'ENVOI

L ORD of my love, to whom in vassalage
    Thy merit hath my duty strongly knit,
To thee I send this written embassage,
To witness duty, not to show my wit :

Duty so great, which wit so poor as mine
May make seem bare, in wanting words to show it,
But that I hope some good conceit of thine
In thy soul's thought, all naked, will bestow it ;

Till whatsoever star that guides my moving
Points on me graciously with fair aspect,
And puts apparel on my tatter'd loving,
To show me worthy of thy sweet respect :

    Then may I dare to boast how I do love thee ;
    Till then not show my head where thou mayst
        prove me.

G

THE LOVER'S NIGHT THOUGHTS

WEARY with toil, I haste me to my bed,
    The dear repose for limbs with travel tired ;
But then begins a journey in my head,
To work my mind, when body's work's expired :

For then my thoughts, from far where I abide,
Intend a zealous pilgrimage to thee,
And keep my drooping eyelids open wide,
Looking on darkness which the blind do see :

Save that my soul's imaginary sight
Presents thy shadow to my sightless view,
Which, like a jewel hung in ghastly night,
Makes black night beauteous and her old face new.

    Lo ! thus, by day my limbs, by night my mind
    For thee and for myself no quiet find.

BY NIGHT AND BY DAY

HOW can I then return in happy plight
    That am debarr'd the benefit of rest?
When day's oppression is not eased by night,
But day by night, and night by day, oppress'd?

And each, though enemies to either's reign,
Do in consent shake hands to torture me ;
The one by toil, the other to complain
How far I toil, still farther off from thee.

I tell the day, to please him thou art bright,
And dost him grace when clouds do blot the
    heaven :
So flatter I the swart-complexion'd night,
When sparkling stars twire not, thou gild'st the
    even.

  But day doth daily draw my sorrows longer,
  And night doth nightly make grief's strength
    seem stronger.

AMOR OMNIA VINCIT

WHEN, in disgrace with fortune and men's
    eyes,
I all alone beweep my outcast state
And trouble deaf heaven with my bootless cries
And look upon myself and curse my fate,

Wishing me like to one more rich in hope,
Featured like him, like him with friends possess'd,
Desiring this man's art and that man's scope,
With what I most enjoy contented least ;

Yet in these thoughts myself almost despising
Haply I think on Thee,—and then my state,
Like to the lark at break of day arising
From sullen earth, sings hymns at heaven's gate ;

    For thy sweet love remember'd such wealth
        brings,
    That then I scorn to change my state with kings.

REMEMBRANCE

WHEN to the sessions of sweet silent thought
    I summon up remembrance of things past,
I sigh the lack of many a thing I sought,
And with old woes new wail my dear time's waste :

Then can I drown an eye, unused to flow,
For precious friends hid in death's dateless night,
And weep afresh love's long since cancell'd woe,
And moan the expense of many a vanish'd sight :

Then can I grieve at grievances foregone,
And heavily from woe to woe tell o'er
The sad account of fore-bemoanéd moan,
Which I new pay as if not paid before.

    But if the while I think on thee, dear Friend,
    All losses are restored, and sorrows end.

ALL-CONTAINING LOVE

THY bosom is endearéd with all hearts,
     Which I by lacking have supposéd dead,
And there reigns love and all love's loving parts,
And all those friends which I thought burléd.

How many a holy and obsequious tear
Hath dear religious love stol'n from mine eye
As interest of the dead, which now appear
But things removed, that hidden in thee lie !

Thou art the grave where buried love doth live,
Hung with the trophies of my lovers gone,
Who all their parts of me to thee did give,
That due of many now is thine alone :

     Their images I loved I view in thee,
     And thou, all they, hast all the all of me.

THE VITAL FORCE

I F thou survive my well-contented day,
    When that churl Death my bones with dust
      shall cover,
And shalt by fortune once more re-survey
These poor rude lines of thy deceaséd lover,

Compare them with the bettering of the time,
And though they be outstripp'd by every pen,
Reserve them for my love, not for their rhyme,
Exceeded by the height of happier men.

O then vouchsafe me but this loving thought :
' Had my friend's Muse grown with this growing
    age,
A dearer birth than this his love had brought,
To march in ranks of better equipage :

    But since he died, and poets better prove,
    Theirs for their style I'll read, his for his love.'

SUNSHINE AND CLOUD

FULL many a glorious morning have I seen
    Flatter the mountain-tops with sovereign eye,
Kissing with golden face the meadows green,
Gilding pale streams with heavenly alchemy;

Anon permit the basest clouds to ride
With ugly rack on his celestial face,
And from the forlorn world his visage hide,
Stealing unseen to west with this disgrace:

Even so my sun one early morn did shine
With all-triumphant splendour on my brow;
But out, alack! he was but one hour mine;
The region cloud hath mask'd him from me now.

Yet him for this my love no whit disdaineth;
    Suns of the world may stain, when heaven's sun
        staineth.

DILEXIT MULTUM

WHY didst thou promise such a beauteous day
    And make me travel forth without my cloak,
To let base clouds o'ertake me in my way,
Hiding thy bravery in their rotten smoke?

'Tis not enough that through the cloud thou break
To dry the rain on my storm-beaten face,
For no man well of such a salve can speak
That heals the wound, and cures not the disgrace :

Nor can thy shame give physic to my grief ;
Though thou repent, yet I have still the loss :
The offender's sorrow lends but weak relief
To him that bears the strong offence's cross.

Ah ! but those tears are pearl which thy love
        sheds,
And they are rich, and ransom all ill deeds.

A CONFESSION

NO more be grieved at that which thou hast
    done :
Roses have thorns, and silver fountains mud ;
Clouds and eclipses stain both moon and sun,
And loathsome canker lives in sweetest bud.

All men make faults, and even I in this,
Authorizing thy trespass with compare,
Myself corrupting, salving thy amiss,
Excusing thy sins more than thy sins are;

For to thy sensual fault I bring in sense—
Thy adverse party is thy advocate—
And 'gainst myself a lawful plea commence :
Such civil war is in my love and hate

    That I an accessary needs must be
    To that sweet thief which sourly robs from me.

ANOTHER CONFESSION

LET me confess that we two must be twain,
  Although our undivided loves are one :
So shall those blots that do with me remain
Without thy help by me be borne alone.

In our two loves there is but one respect,
Though in our lives a separable spite,
Which though it alter not love's sole effect,
Yet doth it steal sweet hours from love's delight.

I may not evermore acknowledge thee
Lest my bewailéd guilt should do thee shame,
Nor thou with public kindness honour me,
Unless thou take that honour from thy name :

  But do not so ; I love thee in such sort
  As, thou being mine, mine is thy good report.

THE RECOMPENSE

AS a decrepit father takes delight
    To see his active child do deeds of youth,
So I, made lame by fortune's dearest spite,
Take all my comfort of thy worth and truth.

For whether beauty, birth, or wealth, or wit,
Or any of these all, or all, or more,
Entitled in thy parts do crownéd sit,
I make my love engrafted to this store :

So then I am not lame, poor, nor despised,
Whilst that this shadow doth such substance give
That I in thy abundance am sufficed,
And by a part of all thy glory live.

   Look, what is best, that best I wish in thee :
   This wish I have ; then ten times happy me !

THE NEW MUSE

HOW can my Muse want subject to invent
    While thou dost breathe, that pour'st into
      my verse
Thine own sweet argument, too excellent
For every vulgar paper to rehearse?

O, give thyself the thanks, if aught in me
Worthy perusal stand against thy sight;
For who's so dumb that cannot write to thee,
When thou thyself dost give invention light?

Be thou the tenth Muse, ten times more in worth
Than those old nine which rhymers invocate;
And he that calls on thee, let him bring forth
Eternal numbers to outlive long date.

  If my slight Muse do please these curious days,
  The pain be mine, but thine shall be the praise.

IDENTITY IN LOVE

O, HOW thy worth with manners may I sing,
    When thou art all the better part of me?
What can mine own praise to mine own self bring?
And what is't but mine own when I praise thee?

Even for this let us divided live,
And our dear love lose name of single one,
That by this separation I may give
That due to thee which thou deserv'st alone.

O Absence, what a torment would'st thou prove,
Were it not thy sour leisure gave sweet leave
To entertain the time with thoughts of love,
Which time and thoughts so sweetly doth deceive,

    And that thou teachest how to make one twain,
    By praising him here who doth hence remain !

ALL FOR LOVE

TAKE all my loves, my Love, yea, take them
   all ;
What hast thou then more than thou hadst before?
No love, my Love, that thou mayst true love call ;
All mine was thine, before thou hadst this more.

Then if for my love thou my love receivest,
I cannot blame thee for my love thou usest ;
But yet be blamed, if thou thyself deceivest
By wilful taste of what thyself refusest.

I do forgive thy robbery, gentle thief,
Although thou steal thee all my poverty;
And yet, love knows, it is a greater grief
To bear love's wrong than hate's known injury.

   Lascivious grace, in whom all ill well shows,
   Kill me with spites; yet we must not be foes.

A PARDON

THOSE petty wrongs that liberty commits,
　　When I am sometime absent from thy heart,
Thy beauty and thy years full well befits,
For still temptation follows where thou art.

Gentle thou art, and therefore to be won,
Beauteous thou art, therefore to be assailéd ;
And when a woman woos, what woman's son
Will sourly leave her till she have prevailéd?

Ay me ! but yet thou mightst my seat forbear,
And chide thy beauty and thy straying youth,
Who lead thee in their riot even there
Where thou art forced to break a twofold truth, —

　　Hers, by thy beauty tempting her to thee,
　　Thine, by thy beauty being false to me.

THEFT NO ROBBERY

THAT thou hast her, it is not all my grief ;
    And yet it may be said I loved her dearly ;
That she hath thee, is of my wailing chief,
A loss in love that touches me more nearly.

Loving offenders, thus I will excuse ye :
Thou dost love her, because thou know'st I love
    her ;
And for my sake even so doth she abuse me,
Suffering my friend for my sake to approve her.

If I lose thee, my loss is my love's gain,
And losing her, my friend hath found that loss ;
Both find each other, and I lose both twain,
And both for my sake lay on me this cross :

    But here's the joy ; my friend and I are one ;
    Sweet flattery ! then she loves but me alone.

H

SHADOW AND TRUTH

WHEN most I wink, then do mine eyes best
    see,
For all the day they view things unrespected;
But when I sleep, in dreams they look on thee,
And darkly bright are bright in dark directed.

Then thou, whose shadow shadows doth make
    bright,
How would thy shadow's form form happy show
To the clear day with thy much clearer light,
When to unseeing eyes thy shade shines so!

How would, I say, mine eyes be blessèd made
By looking on thee in the living day,
When in dead night thy fair imperfect shade
Through heavy sleep on sightless eyes doth stay!

    All days are nights to see till I see thee,
    And nights bright days when dreams do show
        thee me.

SOUL AND BODY

IF the dull substance of my flesh were thought,
　Injurious distance should not stop my way ;
For then, despite of space, I would be brought
From limits far remote, where thou dost stay.

No matter then although my food did stand
Upon the farthest earth removed from thee ;
For nimble thought can jump both sea and land
As soon as think the place where he would be.

But, ah ! thought kills me that I am not thought,
To leap large lengths of miles when thou art gone,
But that, so much of earth and water wrought,
I must attend time's leisure with my moan ;

　Receiving nought by elements so slow
　But heavy tears, badges of either's woe.

SOUL AND BODY

THE other two, slight air and purging fire,
   Are both with thee, wherever I abide ;
The first my thought, the other my desire,
These, present-absent, with swift motion slide.

For when these quicker elements are gone
In tender embassy of love to thee,
My life, being made of four, with two alone
Sinks down to death, oppress'd with melancholy ;

Until life's composition be recured
By those swift messengers return'd from thee,
Who even but now come back again, assured
Of thy fair health, recounting it to me :

  This told, I joy ; but then no longer glad,
  I send them back again and straight grow sad.

IN THE COURT OF LOVE

MINE eye and heart are at a mortal war
    How to divide the conquest of thy sight ;
Mine eye my heart thy picture's sight would bar,
My heart mine eye the freedom of that right.

My heart doth plead that thou in him dost lie,—
A closet never pierced with crystal eyes—
But the defendant doth that plea deny,
And says in him thy fair appearance lies.

To 'cide this title is impanneléd
A quest of thoughts, all tenants to the heart,
And by their verdict is determinéd
The clear eye's moiety and the dear heart's part :

    As thus ; mine eye's due is thy outward part,
    And my heart's right thy inward love of heart.

THE PICTURE AND THE IDEA

BETWIXT mine eye and heart a league is took,
    And each doth good turns now unto the
      other ;
When that mine eye is famish'd for a look,
Or heart in love with sighs himself doth smother,

With my Love's picture then my eye doth feast
And to the painted banquet bids my heart ;
Another time mine eye is my heart's guest
And in his thoughts of love doth share a part:

So, either by thy picture or my love,
Thyself away art present still with me ;
For thou not farther than my thoughts canst move,
And I am still with them and they with thee ;

    Or, if they sleep, thy picture in my sight
    Awakes my heart to heart's and eye's delight.

THE TREASURE OF TREASURES

HOW careful was I, when I took my way,
    Each trifle under truest bars to thrust,
That to my use it might unuséd stay
From hands of falsehood, in sure wards of trust !

But thou, to whom my jewels trifles are,
Most worthy comfort, now my greatest grief,
Thou, best of dearest and mine only care,
Art left the prey of every vulgar thief.

Thee have I not lock'd up in any chest,
Save where thou art not, though I feel thou art,
Within the gentle closure of my breast,
From whence at pleasure thou mayst come and
    part ;

—And even thence thou wilt be stol'n, I fear,
For truth proves thievish for a prize so dear.

A FOREBODING

AGAINST that time, if ever that time come,
　　When I shall see thee frown on my defects,
When-as thy love hath cast his utmost sum,
Call'd to that audit by advised respects ;

Against that time when thou shalt strangely pass
And scarcely greet me with that sun, thine eye,
When love, converted from the thing it was,
Shall reasons find of settled gravity,—

Against that time do I ensconce me here
Within the knowledge of mine own desert,
And this my hand against myself uprear,
To guard the lawful reasons on thy part :

　　To leave poor me thou hast the strength of laws,
　　Since why to love I can allege no cause.

VIA DOLOROSA

HOW heavy do I journey on the way
    When what I seek, my weary travel's end,
Doth teach that ease and that repose to say
' Thus far the miles are measured from thy friend!'

The beast that bears me, tired with my woe,
Plods dully on, to bear that weight in me,
As if by some instinct the wretch did know
His rider loved not speed, being made from thee :

The bloody spur cannot provoke him on
That sometimes anger thrusts into his hide,
Which heavily he answers with a groan
More sharp to me than spurring to his side ;

    For that same groan doth put this in my mind;
    My grief lies onward, and my joy behind.

THE RETURN

THUS can my love excuse the slow offence
    Of my dull bearer when from thee I speed :
From where thou art why should I haste me thence ?
Till I return, of posting is no need.

O, what excuse will my poor beast then find,
When swift extremity can seem but slow ?
Then should I spur, though mounted on the wind ;
In wingéd speed no motion shall I know :

Then can no horse with my desire keep pace ;
Therefore desire, of perfect'st love being made,
Shall neigh—no dull flesh—in his fiery race ;
But love, for love, thus shall excuse my jade ;

    Since from thee going he went wilful-slow,
    Towards thee I'll run, and give him leave to go.

CARUM QUOD RARUM

SO am I as the rich, whose blesséd key
    Can bring him to his sweet up-lockéd treasure,
The which he will not every hour survey,
For blunting the fine point of seldom pleasure.

Therefore are feasts so seldom and so rare,
Since, seldom coming, in the long year set,
Like stones of worth they thinly placéd are,
Or captain jewels in the carcanet.

So is the time that keeps you as my chest,
Or as the wardrobe which the robe doth hide
To make some special instant special-blest
By new unfolding his imprison'd pride.

    Blesséd are you, whose worthiness gives scope,
    Being had, to triumph, being lack'd, to hope.

REALITY AND SHADOW

WHAT is your substance? whereof are you
　　　made,
That millions of strange shadows on you tend?
Since every one hath, every one, one shade,
And you, but one, can every shadow lend.

Describe Adonis, and the counterfeit
Is poorly imitated after you;
On Helen's cheek all art of beauty set,
And you in Grecian tires are painted new:

Speak of the spring and foison of the year;
The one doth shadow of your beauty show,
The other as your bounty doth appear;
And you in every blesséd shape we know :—

　　In all external grace you have some part,
　　But you like none, none you, for constant heart.

THE TRUE AND THE FALSE

O, HOW much more doth beauty beauteous seem,
By that sweet ornament which truth doth
give !
The rose looks fair, but fairer we it deem
For that sweet odour which doth in it live :

The canker-blooms have full as deep a dye
As the perfuméd tincture of the roses,
Hang on such thorns, and play as wantonly
When summer's breath their maskéd buds dis-
closes : '

But, for their virtue only is their show,
They live unwoo'd and unrespected fade,
Die to themselves.   Sweet roses do not so ;
Of their sweet deaths are sweetest odours made :

And so of you, beauteous and lovely youth,
When that shall fade, my verse distils your truth.

EXEGI MONUMENTUM

NOT marble, nor the gilded monuments
    Of princes, shall outlive this powerful rhyme;
But you shall shine more bright in these contents
Than unswept stone besmear'd with sluttish time.

When wasteful war shall statues overturn,
And broils root out the work of masonry,
Nor Mars his sword nor war's quick fire shall burn
The living record of your memory.

Gainst death and all-oblivious enmity
Shall you pace forth ; your praise shall still find
    room
Even in the eyes of all posterity
That wear this world out to the ending doom.

    So, till the judgment that yourself arise,
    You live in this, and dwell in lovers' eyes.

EBB AND FLOW

SWEET Love, renew thy force ; be it not said
  Thy edge should blunter be than appetite,
Which but to-day by feeding is allay'd,
To-morrow sharpen'd in his former might :

So, Love, be thou ; although to-day thou fill
Thy hungry eyes even till they wink with fullness.
To-morrow see again, and do not kill
The spirit of love with a perpetual dullness.

Let this sad interim like the ocean be
Which parts the shore, where two contracted new
Come daily to the banks, that, when they see
Return of love, more blest may be the view ;

  Else call it winter, which being full of care
  Makes summer's welcome thrice more wish'd,
    more rare.

ABSENCE

BEING your slave, what should I do but tend
    Upon the hours and times of your desire?
I have no precious time at all to spend,
Nor services to do, till you require.

Nor dare I chide the world-without-end hour
Whilst I, my sovereign, watch the clock for you,
Nor think the bitterness of absence sour
When you have bid your servant once adieu;

Nor dare I question with my jealous thought
Where you may be, or your affairs suppose,
But, like a sad slave, stay and think of nought
Save, where you are how happy you make those.

  So true a fool is love, that in your will
  Though you do any thing, he thinks no ill.

SUBMISSION ABSOLUTE

THAT god forbid that made me first your slave,
.I should in thought control your times of
pleasure,
Or at your hand the account of hours to crave,
Being your vassal, bound to stay your leisure !

O let me suffer, being at your beck,
The imprison'd absence of your liberty ;
And patience, tame to sufferance, bide each check,
Without accusing you of injury.

Be where you list, your charter is so strong
That you yourself may privilege your time
To what you will ; to you it doth belong
Yourself to pardon of self-doing crime.

I am to wait, though waiting so be hell ;
Not blame your pleasure, be it ill or well.

NIHIL NOVI, NIHIL INAUDITI

IF there be nothing new, but that which is
    Hath been before, how are our brains be-
      guiled,
Which, labouring for invention, bear amiss
The second burden of a former child !

O, that record could with a backward look,
Even of five hundred courses of the sun,
Show me your image in some antique book,
Since mind at first in character was done !

That I might see what the old world could say
To this composéd wonder of your frame ;
Whether we are mended, or whether better they,
Or whether revolution be the same.

    O, sure I am, the wits of former days
    To subjects worse have given admiring praise.

REVOLUTIONS

L IKE as the waves make towards the pebbled
    shore,
So do our minutes hasten to their end ;
Each changing place with that which goes before
In sequent toil all forwards do contend.

Nativity, once in the main of light,
Crawls to maturity, wherewith being crown'd,
Crooked eclipses 'gainst his glory fight,
And Time that gave doth now his gift confound.

Time doth transfix the flourish set on youth
And delves the parallels in beauty's brow,
Feeds on the rarities of nature's truth,
And nothing stands but for his scythe to mow:

    And yet to times in hope my verse shall stand
    Praising thy worth, despite his cruel hand.

ALAS

IS it thy will thy image should keep open
    My heavy eyelids to the weary night ?
Dost thou desire my slumbers should be broken,
While shadows like to thee do mock my sight ?

Is it thy spirit that thou send'st from thee
So far from home into my deeds to pry,
To find out shames and idle hours in me,
The scope and tenour of thy jealousy ?

O, no ! thy love, though much, is not so great :
It is my love that keeps mine eye awake ;
Mine own true love that doth my rest defeat,
To play the watchman ever for thy sake :

    For thee watch I whilst thou dost wake else-
        where,
    From me far off, with others all too near.

A LESSON

SIN of self-love possesseth all mine eye
    And all my soul and all my every part ;
And for this sin there is no remedy,
It is so grounded inward in my heart.

Methinks no face so gracious is as mine,
No shape so true, no truth of such account ;
And for myself mine own worth do define,
As I all other in all worths surmount.

But when my glass shows me myself indeed,
Beated and chopp'd with tann'd antiquity,
Mine own self-love quite contrary I read ;
Self so self-loving were iniquity.

    'Tis thee, myself, that for myself I praise,
    Painting my age with beauty of thy days.

A PROTEST

AGAINST my Love shall be, as I am now,
    With Time's injurious hand crush'd and
      o'erworn ;
When hours have drain'd his blood and fill'd his
  brow
With lines and wrinkles ; when his youthful morn

Hath travell'd on to age's steepy night,
And all those beauties whereof now he's king
Are vanishing or vanish'd out of sight,
Stealing away the treasure of his spring ;

For such a time do I now fortify
Against confounding age's cruel knife,
That he shall never cut from memory
My sweet Love's beauty, though my lover's life :

  His beauty shall in these black lines be seen,
  And they shall live, and he in them still green.

TIME AND LOVE

WHEN I have seen by Time's fell hand de-
 faced
The rich proud cost of outworn buried age ;
When sometime lofty towers I see down-razed,
And brass eternal slave to mortal rage ;

When I have seen the hungry ocean gain
Advantage on the kingdom of the shore,
And the firm soil win of the watery main,
Increasing store with loss, and loss with store ;

When I have seen such interchange of state,
Or state itself confounded to decay,—
Ruin hath taught me thus to ruminate,
That Time will come and take my Love away :

—This thought is as a death, which cannot choose
But weep to have that which it fears to lose.

TIME AND LOVE

SINCE brass, nor stone, nor earth, nor boundless
     sea,
But sad mortality o'er-sways their power,
How with this rage shall beauty hold a plea,
Whose action is no stronger than a flower?

O, how shall summer's honey breath hold out
Against the wreckful siege of battering days,
When rocks impregnable are not so stout,
Nor gates of steel so strong, but Time decays?

O fearful meditation ; where, alack,
Shall Time's best jewel from Time's chest lie hid?
Or what strong hand can hold his swift foot back?
Or who his spoil of beauty can forbid?

    O, none, unless this miracle have might,
    That in black ink my Love may still shine bright.

THE WORLD'S WAY

TIRED with all these, for restful death I cry,—
    As, to behold desert a beggar born,
And needy nothing trimm'd in jollity,
And purest faith unhappily forsworn,

And gilded honour shamefully misplaced,
And maiden virtue rudely strumpeted,
And right perfection wrongfully disgraced,
And strength by limping sway disabled,

And art made tongue-tied by authority,
And folly, doctor-like, controlling skill,
And simple truth miscall'd simplicity,
And captive Good attending captain Ill :

    —Tired with all these, from these would I be
        gone,—
Save that, to die, I leave my Love alone.

THE ONE AND ONLY

AH ! wherefore with infection should he live,
　　And with his presence grace impiety,
That sin by him advantage should achieve
And lace itself with his society ?

Why should false painting imitate his cheek
And steal dead seeing of his living hue ?
Why should poor beauty indirectly seek
Roses of shadow, since his rose is true ?

Why should he live, now Nature bankrupt is,
Beggar'd of blood to blush through lively veins ?
For she hath no exchequer now but his,
And, proud of many, lives upon his gains.

　　O ! him she stores, to show what wealth she had
　　In days long since, before these last so bad.

AGE UNSHAMED

THUS is his cheek the map of days outworn,
 When beauty lived and died as flowers do
  now,
Before these bastard signs of fair were born,
Or durst inhabit on a living brow ;

Before the golden tresses of the dead,
The right of sepulchres, were shorn away
To live a second life on second head ;
Ere beauty's dead fleece made another gay :

In him those holy antique hours are seen,
Without all ornament, itself and true,
Making no summer of another's green,
Robbing no old to dress his beauty new ;

 And him as for a map doth Nature store,
 To show false Art what beauty was of yore.

MEDIO DE FONTE

THOSE parts of thee that the world's eye doth
　　view
Want nothing that the thought of hearts can
　　mend ;
All tongues, the voice of souls, give thee that due,
Uttering bare truth, even so as foes commend.

Thy outward thus with outward praise is crown'd ;
But those same tongues that give thee so thine own
In other accents do this praise confound
By seeing farther than the eye hath shown.

They look into the beauty of thy mind,
And that, in guess, they measure by thy deeds ;
Then, churls, their thoughts, although their eyes
　　were kind,
To thy fair flower add the rank smell of weeds :

　　But why thy odour matcheth not thy show,
　　The solve is this, that thou dost common grow.

INEVITABLE SLANDER

THAT thou art blamed shall not be thy defect,
 For slander's mark was ever yet the fair ;
The ornament of beauty is suspect,
A crow that flies in heaven's sweetest air.

So thou be good, slander doth but approve
Thy worth the greater, being woo'd of time ;
For canker vice the sweetest buds doth love,
And thou present'st a pure unstainéd prime.

Thou hast pass'd by the ambush of young days
Either not assail'd, or victor being charged ;
Yet this thy praise cannot be so thy praise,
To tie up envy evermore enlarged :

 If some suspect of ill mask'd not thy show,
 Then thou alone kingdoms of hearts shouldst
  owe.

THE TRIUMPH OF DEATH

NO longer mourn for me when I am dead
    Than you shall hear the surly sullen bell
Give warning to the world that I am fled
From this vile world, with vilest worms to dwell :

Nay, if you read this line, remember not
The hand that writ it ; for I love you so
That I in your sweet thoughts would be forgot
If thinking on me then should make you woe.

O ! if, I say, you look upon this verse
When I perhaps compounded am with clay,
Do not so much as my poor name rehearse,
But let your love even with my life decay,—

    Lest the wise world should look into your moan,
    And mock you with me after I am gone.

SELF ABASEMENT

O, lest the world should task you to recite
    What merit lived in me, that you should
        love
After my death, dear Love, forget me quite,
For you in me can nothing worthy prove ;

Unless you would devise some virtuous lie
To do more for me than mine own desert,
And hang more praise upon deceaséd I
Than niggard truth would willingly impart :

O, lest your true love may seem false in this,
That you for love speak well of me untrue,
My name be buried where my body is,
And live no more to shame nor me nor you : —

    For I am shamed by that which I bring forth,
    And so should you, to love things nothing worth.

QUATUOR NOVISSIMA

THAT time of year thou mayst in me behold
    When yellow leaves, or none, or few, do hang
Upon those boughs which shake against the cold,
Bare ruin'd choirs, where late the sweet bird
    sang :

In me thou see'st the twilight of such day
As after sunset fadeth in the west,
Which by and by black night doth take away,
Death's second self, that seals up all in rest :

In me thou see'st the glowing of such fire
That on the ashes of his youth doth lie
As the death-bed whereon it must expire,
Consumed with that which it was nourish'd by :—

    This thou perceiv'st, which makes thy love more
        strong,
    To love that well which thou must leave ere
        long.

THE POET'S IMMORTALITY

BUT be contented : when that fell arrest
        Without all bail shall carry me away,
My life hath in this line some interest,
Which for memorial still with thee shall stay.

When thou reviewest this, thou dost review
The very part was consecrate to thee :
The earth can have but earth, which is his due ;
My spirit is thine, the better part of me :

So then thou hast but lost the dregs of life,
The prey of worms, my body being dead,
The coward conquest of a wretch's knife,
Too base of thee to be rememberéd.

    The worth of that is that which it contains,
    And that is this, and this with thee remains.

K

RICH AND POOR

So are you to my thoughts as food to life,
    Or as sweet-season'd showers are to the
        ground ;
And for the peace of you I hold such strife
As 'twixt a miser and his wealth is found ;

Now proud as an enjoyer, and anon
Doubting the filching age will steal his treasure ;
Now counting best to be with you alone,
Then better'd that the world may see my pleasure ;

Sometime all full with feasting on your sight,
And by and by clean starvéd for a look ;
Possessing or pursuing no delight
Save what is had or must from you be took.

    Thus do I pine and surfeit day by day,
      Or gluttoning on all, or all away.

SWEET MONOTONY

WHY is my verse so barren of new pride,
     So far from variation or quick change?
Why with the time do I not glance aside
To new-found methods and to compounds strange?

Why write I still all one, ever the same,
And keep invention in a noted weed,
That every word doth almost tell my name,
Showing their birth and where they did proceed?

O, know, sweet Love, I always write of you,
And you and love are still my argument;
So all my best is dressing old words new,
Spending again what is already spent:

   For as the sun is daily new and old,
   So is my love still telling what is told.

WITH AN ALBUM

THY glass will show thee how thy beauties wear,
   Thy dial how thy precious minutes waste ;
The vacant leaves thy mind's imprint will bear,
And of this book this learning mayst thou taste.

The wrinkles which thy glass will truly show
Of mouthéd graves will give thee memory ;
Thou by thy dial's shady stealth mayst know
Time's thievish progress to eternity.

Look, what thy memory can not contain
Commit to these waste blanks, and thou shalt find
Those children nursed, deliver'd from thy brain,
To take a new acquaintance of thy mind.

  These offices, so oft as thou wilt look,
  Shall profit thee and much enrich thy book.

THE TRUE INSPIRATION

SO oft have I invoked thee for my Muse
    And found such fair assistance in my verse,
As every alien pen hath got my use,
And under thee their poesy disperse.

Thine eyes that taught the dumb on high to sing
And heavy ignorance aloft to fly,
Have added feathers to the learnéd's wing,
And given grace a double majesty.

Yet be most proud of that which I compile,
Whose influence is thine and born of thee :
In others' works thou dost but mend the style,
And arts with thy sweet graces gracéd be ;

But thou art all my art, and dost advance
As high as learning my rude ignorance.

THE IDEAL

WHILST I alone did call upon thy aid,
　　My verse alone had all thy gentle grace,
But now my gracious numbers are decay'd,
And my sick Muse doth give another place.

I grant, sweet Love, thy lovely argument
Deserves the travail of a worthier pen,
Yet what of thee thy poet doth invent
He robs thee of and pays it thee again.

He lends thee virtue, and he stole that word
From thy behaviour ; beauty doth he give
And found it in thy cheek ; he can afford
No praise to thee but what in thee doth live.

　　Then thank him not for that which he doth say,
　　Since what he owes thee thou thyself dost pay.

THE RIVAL DEFIED

O, HOW I faint when I of you do write,
    Knowing a better spirit doth use your name,
And in the praise thereof spends all his might,
To make me tongue-tied, speaking of your fame !

But since your worth, wide as the ocean is,
The humble as the proudest sail doth bear,
My saucy bark inferior far to his
On your broad main doth wilfully appear.

Your shallowest help will hold me up afloat,
Whilst he upon your soundless deep doth ride ;
Or, being wreck'd, I am a worthless boat,
He of tall building and of goodly pride :

    Then if he thrive and I be cast away,
    The worst was this ; my love was my decay.

A PROPHECY

OR I shall live your epitaph to make,
 Or you survive when I in earth am rotten ;
From hence your memory death cannot take,
Although in me each part will be forgotten.

Your name from hence immortal life shall have,
Though I, once gone, to all the world must die :
The earth can yield me but a common grave,
When you entombéd in men's eyes shall lie.

Your monument shall be my gentle verse,
Which eyes not yet created shall o'er-read,
And tongues to be your being shall rehearse
When all the breathers of this world are dead ;

 You still shall live—such virtue hath my pen—
 Where breath most breathes, even in the mouths
  of men.

THE TRUE PRAISE

I GRANT thou wert not married to my Muse,
And therefore mayst without attaint o'erlook
The dedicated words which writers use
Of their fair subject, blessing every book.

Thou art as fair in knowledge as in hue,
Finding thy worth a limit past my praise,
And therefore art enforced to seek anew
Some fresher stamp of the time-bettering days.

And do so, Love ; yet when they have devised
What strainéd touches rhetoric can lend,
Thou truly fair wert truly sympathized
In true plain words by thy true-telling friend ;

And their gross painting might be better used
Where cheeks need blood ; in thee it is abused.

OF HIS SILENCE

I NEVER saw that you did painting need,
    And therefore to your fair no painting set ;
I found, or thought I found, you did exceed
The barren tender of a poet's debt ;

And therefore have I slept in your report,
That you yourself being extant well might show
How far a modern quill doth come too short,
Speaking of worth, what worth in you doth grow.

This silence for my sin you did impute,
Which shall be most my glory, being dumb ;
For I impair not beauty being mute,
When others would give life and bring a tomb.

    There lives more life in one of your fair eyes
    Than both your poets can in praise devise.

LOVE'S ONE WORD

WHO is it that says most? which can say more
    Than this rich praise, that you alone are
      you ?
In whose confine immuréd is the store
Which should example where your equal grew.

Lean penury within that pen doth dwell
That to his subject lends not some small glory ;
But he that writes of you, if he can tell
That you are you, so dignifies his story.

Let him but copy what in you is writ,
Not making worse what nature made so clear,
And such a counterpart shall fame his wit,
Making his style admiréd every where.

  You to your beauteous blessings add a curse,
    Being fond of praise, which makes your praises
    worse.

ELOQUENT SILENCE

MY tongue-tied Muse in manners holds her still
    While comments of your praise, richly com-
        piled,
Reserve their character with golden quill
And precious phrase by all the Muses filed.

I think good thoughts whilst others write good
    words,
And like unletter'd clerk still cry 'Amen'
To every hymn that able spirit affords
In polish'd form of well-refinéd pen.

Hearing you praised, I say ''Tis so, 'tis true,'
And to the most of praise add something more ;
But that is in my thought, whose love to you,
Though words come hindmost, holds his rank
    before.

    Then others for the breath of words respect,
    Me for my dumb thoughts, speaking in effect.

JEALOUSY

WAS it the proud full sail of his great verse,
    Bound for the prize of all-too-precious you,
That did my ripe thoughts in my brain inhearse,
Making their tomb the womb wherein they grew ?

Was it his spirit, by spirits taught to write
Above a mortal pitch, that struck me dead ?
No, neither he, nor his compeers by night
Giving him aid, my verse astonishéd.

He, nor that affable familiar ghost
Which nightly gulls him with intelligence,
As victors of my silence cannot boast ;
I was not sick of any fear from thence :

    But when your countenance fill'd up his line,
    Then lack'd I matter; that enfeebled mine.

A RENUNCIATION

FAREWELL! thou art too dear for my
    possessing,
And like enough thou know'st thy estimate :
The charter of thy worth gives thee releasing ;
My bonds in thee are all determinate.

For how do I hold thee but by thy granting ?
And for that riches where is my deserving ?
The cause of this fair gift in me is wanting,
And so my patent back again is swerving.

Thyself thou gav'st, thy own worth then not
    knowing,
Or me, to whom thou gav'st it, else mistaking ;
So thy great gift, upon misprision growing,
Comes home again, on better judgment making.

Thus have I had thee, as a dream doth flatter ;
In sleep a king, but waking no such matter.

LOVE'S EXCUSES

WHEN thou shalt be disposed to set me light,
　　And place my merit in the eye of scorn,
Upon thy side against myself I'll fight
And prove thee virtuous, though thou art forsworn.

With mine own weakness being best acquainted,
Upon thy part I can set down a story
Of faults conceal'd, wherein I am attainted,
That thou in losing me shalt win much glory :

And I by this will be a gainer too ;
For bending all my loving thoughts on thee,
The injuries that to myself I do,
Doing thee vantage, double-vantage me.

　Such is my love, to thee I so belong,
　That for thy right myself will bear all wrong.

LOVE'S EXCUSES

SAY that thou didst forsake me for some fault,
    And I will comment upon that offence ;
Speak of my lameness, and I straight will halt,
Against thy reasons making no defence.

Thou canst not, Love, disgrace me half so ill,
To set a form upon desiréd change,
As I'll myself disgrace : knowing thy will,
I will acquaintance strangle and look strange,

Be absent from thy walks, and in my tongue
Thy sweet belovéd name no more shall dwell,
Lest I, too much profane, should do it wrong
And haply of our old acquaintance tell.

For thee against myself I'll vow debate,
For I must ne'er love him whom thou dost hate.

AN APPEAL OF DESPAIR

THEN hate me when thou wilt ; if ever, now ;
  Now, while the world is bent my deeds to
    cross,
Join with the spite of fortune, make me bow,
And do not drop in for an after-loss :

Ah, do not, when my heart hath 'scaped this
    sorrow,
Come in the rearward of a conquer'd woe ;
Give not a windy night a rainy morrow,
To linger out a purposed overthrow.

If thou wilt leave me, do not leave me last
When other petty griefs have done their spite,
But in the onset come ; so shall I taste
At first the very worst of fortune's might ;

  And other strains of woe, which now seem woe,
  Compared with loss of thee will not seem so.

I.

ALL THINGS IN LOVE

SOME glory in their birth, some in their skill,
 Some in their wealth, some in their bodies'
  force,
Some in their garments, though new-fangled ill,
Some in their hawks and hounds, some in their
 horse :

And every humour hath his adjunct pleasure,
Wherein it finds a joy above the rest :
But these particulars are not my measure ;
All these I better in one general best.

Thy love is better than high birth to me,
Richer than wealth, prouder than garments' cost,
Of more delight than hawks or horses be ;
And having thee, of all men's pride I boast :

 Wretched in this alone, that thou mayst take
 All this away and me most wretched make.

THE SOURCE OF LIFE

B UT do thy worst to steal thyself away,
    For term of life thou art assuréd mine,
And life no longer than thy love will stay,
For it depends upon that love of thine.

Then need I not to fear the worst of wrongs,
When in the least of them my life hath end.
I see a better state to me belongs
Than that which on thy humour doth depend ;

Thou canst not vex me with inconstant mind,
Since that my life on thy revolt doth lie.
—O what a happy title do I find,
Happy to have thy love, happy to die !

But what's so blesséd-fair that fears no blot ?
Thou mayst be false, and yet I know it not.

TRUST AND MISTRUST

S O shall I live, supposing thou art true,
　　Like a deceivéd husband ; so love's face
May still seem love to me, though alter'd new ;
Thy looks with me, thy heart in other place :

For there can live no hatred in thine eye,
Therefore in that I cannot know thy change.
In many's looks the false heart's history
Is writ in moods and frowns and wrinkles strange ;

But heaven in thy creation did decree
That in thy face sweet love should ever dwell ;
Whate'er thy thoughts or thy heart's workings be
Thy looks should nothing thence but sweetness tell.

　　How like Eve's apple doth thy beauty grow,
　　If thy sweet virtue answer not thy show !

THE LIFE WITHOUT PASSION

THEY that have power to hurt and will do none,
　That do not do the thing they most do show,
Who, moving others, are themselves as stone,
Unmovéd, cold, and to temptation slow,—

They rightly do inherit heaven's graces
And husband nature's riches from expense ;
They are the lords and owners of their faces,
Others but stewards of their excellence.

The summer's flower is to the summer sweet,
Though to itself it only live and die :
But if that flower with base infection meet,
The basest weed outbraves his dignity :

　For sweetest things turn sourest by their deeds ;
　Lilies that fester smell far worse than weeds.

THE VIRTUE OF BEAUTY

HOW sweet and lovely dost thou make the
    shame
Which, like a canker in the fragrant rose,
Doth spot the beauty of thy budding name !
O, in what sweets dost thou thy sins enclose !

That tongue that tells the story of thy days,
Making lascivious comments on thy sport,
Cannot dispraise but in a kind of praise ;
Naming thy name blesses an ill report.

O, what a mansion have those vices got
Which for their habitation chose out thee,
Where beauty's veil doth cover every blot,
And all things turn to fair that eyes can see !

    Take heed, dear heart, of this large privilege ;
    The hardest knife ill-used doth lose his edge.

THE POWER OF BEAUTY

SOME say thy fault is youth, some wantonness,
　　Some say thy grace is youth and gentle sport;
Both grace and faults are loved of more and less;
Thou mak'st faults graces that to thee resort.

As on the finger of a thronéd queen
The basest jewel will be well esteem'd,
So are those errors that in thee are seen
To truths translated and for true things deem'd.

How many lambs might the stern wolf betray,
If like a lamb he could his looks translate!
How many gazers mightst thou lead away,
If thou wouldst use the strength of all thy state!

　But do not so; I love thee in such sort
　As, thou being mine, mine is thy good report.

ABSENCE FROM HIS LOVE

HOW like a winter hath my absence been
  From thee, the pleasure of the fleeting year !
What freezings have I felt, what dark days seen !
What old December's bareness every where !

And yet this time removed was summer's time ;
The teeming autumn, big with rich increase,
Bearing the wanton burden of the prime,
Like widow'd wombs after their lords' decease :

Yet this abundant issue seem'd to me
But hope of orphans and unfather'd fruit ;
For summer and his pleasures wait on thee,
And, thou away, the very birds are mute ;

 Or, if they sing, 'tis with so dull a cheer
 That leaves look pale, dreading the winter's near.

THE GARDEN OF LOVE

FROM you have I been absent in the spring,
　　When proud-pied April dress'd in all his trim
Hath put a spirit of youth in every thing,
That heavy Saturn laugh'd and leap'd with him.

Yet nor the lays of birds, nor the sweet smell
Of different flowers in odour and in hue,
Could make me any summer's story tell,
Or from their proud lap pluck them where they
　　grew ;

Nor did I wonder at the lily's white,
Nor praise the deep vermilion in the rose ;
They were but sweet, but figures of delight,
Drawn after you, you pattern of all those.

　　Yet seem'd it winter still, and, you away,
　　As with your shadow I with these did play :

THE GARDEN OF LOVE

THE forward violet thus did I chide :
    Sweet thief, whence didst thou steal thy sweet
        that smells,
If not from my Love's breath?   The purple pride
Which on thy soft cheek for complexion dwells
In my Love's veins thou hast too grossly dyed.

The lily I condemnéd for thy hand,
And buds of marjoram had stol'n thy hair :
The roses fearfully on thorns did stand,
One blushing shame, another white despair ;

A third, nor red nor white, had stol'n of both
And to his robbery had annex'd thy breath ;
But, for his theft, in pride of all his growth
A vengeful canker eat him up to death.

    More flowers I noted, yet I none could see
    But sweet or colour it had stol'n from thee.

A REAWAKENING

WHERE art thou, Muse, that thou forget'st so
    long
To speak of that which gives thee all thy might?
Spend'st thou thy fury on some worthless song
Darkening thy power to lend base subjects light?

Return, forgetful Muse, and straight redeem
In gentle numbers time so idly spent;
Sing to the ear that doth thy lays esteem
And gives thy pen both skill and argument.

Rise, resty Muse, my Love's sweet face survey,
If Time have any wrinkle graven there;
If any, be a satire to decay,
And make Time's spoils despiséd every where:

    Give my Love fame faster than Time wastes
        life;
    So thou prevent'st his scythe and crooked knife.

INVOCATION

O TRUANT Muse, what shall be thy amends
    For thy neglect of truth in beauty dyed?
Both truth and beauty on my Love depends;
So dost thou too, and therein dignified.

Make answer, Muse: wilt thou not haply say,
' Truth needs no colour, with his colour fix'd;
Beauty no pencil, beauty's truth to lay;
But best is best, if never intermix'd?'

Because he needs no praise, wilt thou be dumb?
Excuse not silence so; for't lies in thee
To make him much outlive a gilded tomb,
And to be praised of ages yet to be.

    Then do thy office, Muse; I teach thee how
    To make him seem long hence as he shows now.

SILENT ADORATION

MY love is strengthen'd, though more weak in
    seeming ;
I love not less, though less the show appear :
That love is merchandized whose rich esteeming
The owner's tongue doth publish every where.

Our love was new and then but in the spring
When I was wont to greet it with my lays,
As Philomel in summer's front doth sing
And stops her pipe in growth of riper days :

Not that the summer is less pleasant now
Than when her mournful hymns did hush the
    night,
But that wild music burthens every bough
And sweets grown common lose their dear delight.

    Therefore like her I sometime hold my tongue,
    Because I would not dull you with my song.

WEAK WORDS

A LACK, what poverty my Muse brings forth,
    That having such a scope to show her pride,
The argument all bare is of more worth
Than when it hath my added praise beside !

O blame me not, if I no more can write !
Look in your glass, and there appears a face
That over-goes my blunt invention quite,
Dulling my lines and doing me disgrace.

Were it not sinful then, striving to mend,
To mar the subject that before was well ?
For to no other pass my verses tend
Than of your graces and your gifts to tell ;

    And more, much more, than in my verse can sit
    Your own glass shows you when you look in it.

THE EVER-YOUTHFUL

TO me, fair friend, you never can be old,
　For as you were when first your eye I eyed,
Such seems your beauty still.　Three winters cold
Have from the forests shook three summers' pride,

Three beauteous springs to yellow autumn turn'd
In process of the seasons have I seen,
Three April perfumes in three hot Junes burn'd,
Since first I saw you fresh, which yet are green.

Ah ! yet doth beauty, like a dial-hand,
Steal from his figure, and no pace perceived ;
So your sweet hue, which methinks still doth stand,
Hath motion, and mine eye may be deceived :

　For fear of which, hear this, thou age unbred ;
　Ere you were born was beauty's summer dead.

FAIR, KIND, AND TRUE

LET not my love be call'd idolatry,
　　Nor my belovéd as an idol show,
Since all alike my songs and praises be
To one, of one, still such, and ever so.

Kind is my love to-day, to-morrow kind,
Still constant in a wondrous excellence ;
Therefore my verse to constancy confined,
One thing expressing, leaves out difference.

'Fair, kind, and true' is all my argument,
　Fair, kind, and true' varying to other words ;
And in this change is my invention spent,
Three themes in one, which wondrous scope
　　affords.

　'Fair, kind, and true,' have often lived alone,
　Which three till now never kept seat in one.

THE BEAUTY OF BEAUTIES

WHEN in the chronicle of wasted time
    I see descriptions of the fairest wights,
And beauty making beautiful old rhyme
In praise of ladies dead and lovely knights ;

Then, in the blazon of sweet beauty's best,
Of hand, of foot, of lip, of eye, of brow,
I see their antique pen would have express'd
Even such a beauty as you master now.

So all their praises are but prophecies
Of this our time, all you prefiguring ;
And, for they look'd but with divining eyes,
They had not skill enough your worth to sing :

    For we, which now behold these present days,
    Have eyes to wonder, but lack tongues to praise.

M

AMOR CONTRA MUNDUM

NOT mine own fears, nor the prophetic soul
    Of the wide world dreaming on things to
      come
Can yet the lease of my true love control,
Supposed as forfeit to a confined doom.

The mortal moon hath her eclipse endured,
And the sad augurs mock their own presage ;
Incertainties now crown themselves assured,
And peace proclaims olives of endless age.

Now with the drops of this most balmy time
My love looks fresh, and Death to me subscribes,
Since, spite of him, I'll live in this poor rhyme,
While he insults o'er dull and speechless tribes :

    And thou in this shalt find thy monument,
    When tyrants' crests and tombs of brass are
      spent.

THE EVER NEW

WHAT'S in the brain that ink may character
    Which hath not figured to thee my true
      spirit?
What's new to speak, what new to register,
That may express my love or thy dear merit?

Nothing, sweet boy; but yet, like prayers divine,
I must each day say o'er the very same,
Counting no old thing old, thou mine, I thine,
Even as when first I hallow'd thy fair name.

So that eternal love in love's fresh case
Weighs not the dust and injury of age,
Nor gives to necessary wrinkles place,
But makes antiquity for aye his page,

    Finding the first conceit of love there bred
    Where time and outward form would show it
      dead.

PROTESTATION

O, NEVER say that I was false of heart,
    Though absence seem'd my flame to
        qualify.
As easy might I from myself depart
As from my soul, which in thy breast doth lie :

That is my home of love : if I have ranged,
Like him that travels I return again,
Just to the time, not with the time exchanged,
So that myself bring water for my stain.

Never believe, though in my nature reign'd
All frailties that besiege all kinds of blood,
That it could so preposterously be stain'd,
To leave for nothing all thy sum of good ;

    For nothing this wide universe I call,
    Save thou, my rose ; in it thou art my all.

AN APOLOGY

ALAS, 'tis true I have gone here and there
     And made myself a motley to the view,
Gored mine own thoughts, sold cheap what is most
     dear ;
Made old offences of affections new ;

Most true it is that I have look'd on truth
Askance and strangely : but, by all above,
These blenches gave my heart another youth,
And worse essays proved thee my best of love.

Now all is done, have what shall have no end :
Mine appetite I never more will grind
On newer proof, to try an older friend,
A god in love, to whom I am confined :—

   Then give me welcome, next my heaven the best,
   Even to thy pure and most most loving breast.

THE PLAYER'S DEGRADATION

O, FOR my sake do you with fortune chide
    The guilty goddess of my harmful deeds,
That did not better for my life provide
Than public means which public manners breeds.

Thence comes it that my name receives a brand,
And almost thence my nature is subdued
To what it works in, like the dyer's hand :
Pity me then and wish I were renew'd ;

Whilst, like a willing patient, I will drink
Potions of eisel 'gainst my strong infection ;
No bitterness that I will bitter think,
Nor double penance, to correct correction.

    Pity me then, dear friend, and I assure ye
    Even that your pity is enough to cure me.

THE WORLD WELL LOST

YOUR love and pity doth the impression fill
    Which vulgar scandal stamp'd upon my
        brow ;
For what care I who calls me well or ill,
So you o'er-green my bad, my good allow ?

You are my all the world, and I must strive
To know my shames and praises from your tongue ;
None else to me, nor I to none alive,
That my steel'd sense or changes right or wrong.

In so profound abysm I throw all care
Of others' voices, that my adder's sense
To critic and to flatterer stoppéd are.
Mark how with my neglect I do dispense :

    You are so strongly in my purpose bred
    That all the world besides, methinks, are dead.

THE OMNIPRESENT VISION

SINCE I left you, mine eye is in my mind;
    And that which governs me to go about
Doth part his function and is partly blind,
Seems seeing, but effectually is out;

For it no form delivers to the heart
Of bird, of flower, or shape, which it doth latch:
Of his quick objects hath the mind no part,
Nor his own vision holds what it doth catch;

For if it see the rudest or gentlest sight,
The most sweet favour or deformed'st creature,
The mountain or the sea, the day or night,
The crow or dove, it shapes them to your feature:

    Incapable of more, replete with you,
    My most true mind thus makes mine eye untrue.

EYE FLATTERY

OR whether doth my mind, being crown'd with
    you,
Drink up the monarch's plague, this flattery?
Or whether shall I say, mine eye saith true,
And that your love taught it this alchemy,

To make of monsters and things indigest
Such cherubins as your sweet self resemble,
Creating every bad a perfect best,
As fast as objects to his beams assemble?

O, 'tis the first ; 'tis flattery in my seeing,
And my great mind most kingly drinks it up :
Mine eye well knows what with his gust is 'greeing,
And to his palate doth prepare the cup :

    If it be poison'd, 'tis the lesser sin
    That mine eye loves it and doth first begin.

THE GROWTH OF LOVE

THOSE lines that I before have writ do lie,
  Even those that said I could not love you
    dearer :
Yet then my judgment knew no reason why
My most full flame should afterwards burn clearer.

But reckoning time, whose million'd accidents
Creep in 'twixt vows, and change decrees of kings,
Tan sacred beauty, blunt the sharp'st intents,
Divert strong minds to the course of altering
    things ;

Alas, why, fearing of time's tyranny,
Might I not then say ' Now I love you best,'
When I was certain o'er incertainty,
Crowning the present, doubting of the rest ?

Love is a babe ; then might I not say so,
To give full growth to that which still doth grow ?

127

TRUE LOVE

L ET me not to the marriage of true minds
    Admit impediments.   Love is not love
Which alters when it alteration finds,
Or bends with the remover to remove :

O no ! it is an ever-fixéd mark
That looks on tempests and is never shaken ;
It is the star to every wandering bark,
Whose worth's unknown, although his height be
    taken.

Love's not Time's fool, though rosy lips and cheeks
Within his bending sickle's compass come ;
Love alters not with his brief hours and weeks,
But bears it out even to the edge of doom.

If this be error and upon me proved,
I never writ, nor no man ever loved.

A SELF ACCUSATION

ACCUSE me thus : that I have scanted all
    Wherein I should your great deserts repay,
Forgot upon your dearest love to call,
Whereto all bonds do tie me day by day ;

That I have frequent been with unknown minds
And given to time your own dear-purchased right ;
That I have hoisted sail to all the winds
Which should transport me farthest from your
    sight.

Book both my wilfulness and errors down
And on just proof surmise accumulate ;
Bring me within the level of your frown,
But shoot not at me in your waken'd hate ;

    Since my appeal says, I did strive to prove
    The constancy and virtue of your love.

SICK PASSION

LIKE as, to make our appetites more keen,
　　With eager compounds we our palate urge ;
As, to prevent our maladies unseen,
We sicken, to shun sickness, when we purge :

Even so, being full of your ne'er-cloying sweetness,
To bitter sauces did I frame my feeding,
And, sick of welfare, found a kind of meetness
To be diseased ere that there was true needing.

Thus policy in love, to anticipate
The ills that were not, grew to faults assured ;
And brought to medicine a healthful state,
Which, rank of goodness, would by ill be cured :

　　But thence I learn, and find the lesson true,
　　Drugs poison him that so fell sick of you.

GOOD FROM EVIL

WHAT potions have I drunk of Siren tears,
  Distill'd from limbecks foul as hell within,
Applying fears to hopes and hopes to fears,
Still losing when I saw myself to win !

What wretched errors hath my heart committed,
Whilst it hath thought itself so blessèd never !
How have mine eyes out of their spheres been fitted
In the distraction of this madding fever !

O benefit of ill ! now I find true
That better is by evil still made better ;
And ruin'd love, when it is built anew,
Grows fairer than at first, more strong, far greater.

 So I return rebuked to my content,
 And gain by ill thrice more than I have spent.

AMANTIUM IRAE

THAT you were once unkind befriends me now,
    And for that sorrow which I then did feel
Needs must I under my transgression bow,
Unless my nerves were brass or hammer'd steel.

For if you were by my unkindness shaken
As I by yours, you've pass'd a hell of time,
And I, a tyrant, have no leisure taken
To weigh how once I suffer'd in your crime.

O that our night of woe might have remember'd
My deepest sense, how hard true sorrow hits,
And soon to you, as you to me, then tender'd
The humble salve which wounued bosoms fits !

    But that your trespass now becomes a fee ;
    Mine ransoms yours, and yours must ransom me.

DE PROFUNDIS

'TIS better to be vile than vile esteem'd,
      When not to be receives reproach of being,
And the just pleasure lost which is so deem'd
Not by our feeling but by others' seeing :

For why should others' false adulterate eyes
Give salutation to my sportive blood?
Or on my frailties why are frailer spies,
Which in their wills count bad what I think good?

No, I am that I am, and they that level
At my abuses reckon up their own :
I may be straight, though they themselves be bevel ;
By their rank thoughts my deeds must not be
      shown;

   Unless this general evil they maintain,
   All men are bad, and in their badness reign.

THE TABLETS OF THE MIND

THY gift, thy tables, are within my brain
   Full character'd with lasting memory,
Which shall above that idle rank remain
· Beyond all date, even to eternity ;

Or at the least, so long as brain and heart
Have faculty by nature to subsist ;
Till each to razed oblivion yield his part
Of thee, thy record never can be miss'd.

That poor retention could not so much hold,
Nor need I tallies thy dear love to score ;
Therefore to give them from me was I bold,
To trust those tables that receive thee more :

  To keep an adjunct to remember thee
  Were to import forgetfulness in me.

DEFIANCE TO TIME

NO, Time, thou shalt not boast that I do change :
 Thy pyramids built up with newer might
To me are nothing novel, nothing strange ;
They are but dressings of a former sight.

Our dates are brief, and therefore we admire
What thou dost foist upon us that is old,
And rather make them born to our desire
Than think that we before have heard them told.

Thy registers and thee I both defy,
Not wondering at the present nor the past,
For thy records and what we see do lie,
Made more or less by thy continual haste.

 This I do vow and this shall ever be ;
 I will be true, despite thy scythe and thee.

THE TRUE STATESMANSHIP

I F my dear love were but the child of state,
  It might for Fortune's bastard be unfather'd,
As subject to Time's love or to Time's hate,
Weeds among weeds, or flowers with flowers
  gather'd.

No, it was builded far from accident ;
It suffers not in smiling pomp, nor falls
Under the blow of thrallèd discontent,
Whereto the inviting time our fashion calls :

It fears not policy, that heretic,
Which works on leases of short-number'd hours,
But all alone stands hugely politic,
That it nor grows with heat nor drowns with showers.

  To this I witness call the fools of time,
  Which die for goodness, who have lived for crime.

THE FREEMAN OF LOVE

WERE'T aught to me I bore the canopy,
    With my extern the outward honouring,
Or laid great bases for eternity,
Which prove more short than waste or ruining?

Have I not seen dwellers on form and favour
Lose all, and more, by paying too much rent,
For compound sweet foregoing simple savour,
Pitiful thrivers, in their gazing spent?

No, let me be obsequious in thy heart,
And take thou my oblation, poor but free,
Which is not mix'd with seconds, knows no art,
But mutual render, only me for thee.

Hence, thou suborn'd informer! a true soul,
When most impeach'd, stands least in thy control.

O CRUDELIS ADHUC

O THOU, my lovely boy, who in thy power
  Dost hold Time's fickle glass, his sickle, hour ;
Who hast by waning grown, and therein show'st
Thy lovers withering as thy sweet self grow'st ;
If Nature, sovereign mistress over wrack,
As thou goest onwards, still will pluck thee back,
She keeps thee to this purpose, that her skill
May time disgrace and wretched minutes kill.
Yet fear her, O thou minion of her pleasure !
She may detain, but not still keep, her treasure :
Her audit, though delay'd, answer'd must be,
And her quietus is—to render Thee.

OF HIS LADY LOVE

IN the old age black was not counted fair,
　　Or if it were, it bore not beauty's name ;
But now is black beauty's successive heir,
And beauty slander'd with a bastard shame :

For since each hand hath put on nature's power,
Fairing the foul with art's false borrow'd face,
Sweet beauty hath no name, no holy bower,
But is profaned, if not lives in disgrace.

Therefore my mistress' brows are raven black,
Her eyes so suited, and they mourners seem
At such who, not born fair, no beauty lack,
Slandering creation with a false esteem :

　　Yet so they mourn, becoming of their woe,
　　That every tongue says, beauty should look so.

AT THE SPINNET

HOW oft, when thou, my music, music play'st,
 Upon that blessèd wood whose motion
  sounds
With thy sweet fingers, when thou gently sway'st
The wiry concord that mine ear confounds,

Do I envy those jacks that nimble leap
To kiss the tender inward of thy hand,
Whilst my poor lips, which should that harvest reap,
At the wood's boldness by thee blushing stand !

To be so tickled, they would change their state
And situation with those dancing chips,
O'er whom thy fingers walk with gentle gait,
Making dead wood more blest than living lips

 Since saucy jacks so happy are in this,
 Give them thy fingers, me thy lips to kiss.

BEHIND THE VEIL

THE expense of spirit in a waste of shame
Is lust in action ; and till action, lust
Is perjured, murderous, bloody, full of blame,
Savage, extreme, rude, cruel, not to trust,

Enjoy'd no sooner but despiséd straight ;
Past reason hunted, and no sooner had,
Past reason hated, as a swallow'd bait
On purpose laid to make the taker mad ;

Mad in pursuit and in possession so ;
Had, having, and in quest to have, extreme ;
A bliss in proof, and proved, a very woe ;
Before, a joy proposed ; behind, a dream.

—All this the world well knows ; yet none knows
    well
To shun the heaven that leads men to this hell.

TRUTH WITHOUT DISGUISE

M Y mistress' eyes are nothing like the sun ;
 Coral is far more red than her lips' red ;
If snow be white, why then her breasts are dun ;
If hairs be wires, black wires grow on her head.

I have seen roses damask'd, red and white,
But no such roses see I in her cheeks ;
And in some perfumes is there more delight
Than in the breath that from my mistress reeks.

I love to hear her speak, yet well I know
That music hath a far more pleasing sound ;
I grant I never saw a goddess go ;
My mistress, when she walks, treads on the ground :

 And yet, by heaven, I think my Love as rare
 As any she belied with false compare.

THE MISTRESS

THOU art as tyrannous, so as thou art,
　　As those whose beauties proudly make them
　　　　cruel ;
For well thou know'st to my dear doting heart
Thou art the fairest and most precious jewel.

Yet, in good faith, some say that thee behold,
Thy face hath not the power to make love groan :
To say they err I dare not be so bold,
Although I swear it to myself alone.

And, to be sure that is not false I swear,
A thousand groans, but thinking on thy face,
One on another's neck, do witness bear
Thy black is fairest in my judgment's place.

　　In nothing art thou black save in thy deeds,
　　And thence this slander, as I think, proceeds

THE MOURNER'S HOPE

THINE eyes I love, and they, as pitying me,
Knowing thy heart torments me with disdain,
Have put on black, and loving mourners be,
Looking with pretty ruth upon my pain.

And truly not the morning sun of heaven
Better becomes the gray cheeks of the east,
Nor that full star that ushers-in the even
Doth half that glory to the sober west,

As those two mourning eyes become thy face :
O, let it then as well beseem thy heart
To mourn for me, since mourning doth thee grace,
And suit thy pity like in every part.

Then will I swear beauty herself is black
And all they foul that thy complexion lack.

FAITH AND UNFAITH

BESHREW that heart that makes my heart to
    groan
For that deep wound it gives my friend and me!
Is't not enough to torture me alone,
But slave to slavery my sweet'st friend must be?

Me from myself thy cruel eye hath taken,
And my next self thou, harder, hast engross'd :
Of him, myself, and thee, I am forsaken ;
A torment thrice threefold thus to be cross'd.

Prison my heart in thy steel bosom's ward,
But then my friend's heart let my poor heart bail ;
Whoe'er keeps me, let my heart be his guard ;
Thou canst not then use rigour in my gaol :

And yet thou wilt ; for I, being pent in thee,
Perforce am thine, and all that is in me.

SUBTLETIES OF LOVE

SO, now I have confess'd that he is thine,
    And I myself am mortgaged to thy will,
Myself I'll forfeit, so that other mine
Thou wilt restore, to be my comfort still :

But thou wilt not, nor he will not be free,
For thou art covetous and he is kind ;
He learn'd but surety-like to write for me
Under that bond that him as fast doth bind.

The statute of thy beauty thou wilt take,
Thou usurer, that put'st forth all to use,
And sue a friend came debtor for my sake ;
So him I lose through my unkind abuse.

    Him have I lost ; thou hast both him and me :
    He pays the whole, and yet am I not free.

WILLIAM SHAKESPEARE

WHOEVER hath her wish, thou hast thy 'Will,'
    And 'Will' to boot, and 'Will' in overplus ;
More than enough am I that vex thee still,
To thy sweet will making addition thus.

Wilt thou, whose will is large and spacious,
Not once vouchsafe to hide my will in thine ?
Shall will in others seem right gracious,
And in my will no fair acceptance shine ?

The sea, all water, yet receives rain still
And in abundance addeth to his store ;
So thou, being rich in ' Will,' add to thy ' Will '
One will of mine, to make thy large ' Will ' more.

    Let no unkind, no fair beseechers kill ;
    Think all but one, and me in that one ' Will.'

THE SAME

I F thy soul check thee that I come so near,
  Swear to thy blind soul that I was thy 'Will,'
And will, thy soul knows, is admitted there ;
Thus far for love my love-suit, Sweet, fulfil.

'Will' will fulfil the treasure of thy love,
Ay, fill it full with wills, and my will one.
In things of great receipt with ease we prove
Among a number one is reckon'd none :

Then in the number let me pass untold,
Though in thy stores' account I one must be ;
For nothing hold me, so it please thee hold
That nothing me, a something sweet to thee :

  Make but my name thy love, and love that still,
  And then thou lovest me, for my name is 'Will.'

BLIND LOVE

THOU blind fool, Love, what dost thou to mine
    eyes,
That they behold, and see not what they see?
They know what beauty is, see where it lies,
Yet what the best is take the worst to be.

If eyes corrupt by over-partial looks
Be anchor'd in the day where all men ride,
Why of eyes' falsehood hast thou forgéd hooks,
Whereto the judgment of my heart is tied?

(private)
Why should my heart think that a several plot
Which my heart knows the wide world's common
    place?
Or mine eyes seeing this, say this is not,
To put fair truth upon so foul a face?

  In things right true my heart and eyes have err'd,
  And to this false plague are they now transferr'd.

CHERISHED FALSEHOOD

WHEN my Love swears that she is made of
    truth
I do believe her, though I know she lies,
That she might think me some untutor'd youth,
Unlearnéd in the world's false subtleties.

Thus vainly thinking that she thinks me young,
Although she knows my days are past the best,
Simply I credit her false-speaking tongue :
On both sides thus is simple truth suppress'd.

But wherefore says she not she is unjust ?
And wherefore say not I that I am old ?
O, love's best habit is in seeming trust,
And age in love loves not to have years told :

  Therefore I lie with her and she with me,
  And in our faults by lies we flatter'd be.

HOPE AGAINST HOPE

O, CALL not me to justify the wrong
    That thy unkindness lays upon my heart ;
Wound me not with thine eye but with thy tongue ;
Use power with power and slay me not by art.

Tell me thou lov'st elsewhere, but in my sight,
Dear heart, forbear to glance thine eye aside :
What need'st thou wound with cunning, when thy
    might
Is more than my o'er-press'd defence can bide ?

Let me excuse thee : ah ! my Love well knows
Her pretty looks have been mine enemies,
And therefore from my face she turns my foes,
That they elsewhere might dart their injuries :

    Yet do not so ; but since I am near slain,
    Kill me outright with looks and rid my pain.

A LAST PLEA

BE wise as thou art cruel; do not press
  My tongue-tied patience with too much dis-
    dain;
Lest sorrow lend me words and words express
The manner of my pity-wanting pain.

If I might teach thee wit, better it were,
Though not to love, yet, Love, to tell me so;
As testy sick men, when their deaths be near,
No news but health from their physicians know;

For if I should despair, I should grow mad,
And in my madness might speak ill of thee:
Now this ill-wresting world is grown so bad,
Mad slanderers by mad ears believéd be.

  That I may not be so, nor thou belied,
  Bear thine eyes straight, though thy proud heart
    go wide.

LOVE IN UNLOVELINESS

IN faith, I do not love thee with mine eyes,
    For they in thee a thousand errors note;
But 'tis my heart that loves what they despise,
Who in despite of view is pleased to dote;

Nor are mine ears with thy tongue's tune delighted,
Nor tender feeling, to base touches prone,
Nor taste, nor smell, desire to be invited
To any sensual feast with thee alone:

But my five wits nor my five senses can
Dissuade one foolish heart from serving thee,
Who leaves unsway'd the likeness of a man,
Thy proud heart's slave and vassal wretch to be:

    Only my plague thus far I count my gain,
    That she that makes me sin awards me pain.

APPLES OF THE DEAD SEA

LOVE is my sin and thy dear virtue hate,
   Hate of my sin, grounded on sinful loving :
O, but with mine compare thou thine own state,
And thou shalt find it merits not reproving ;

Or, if it do, not from those lips of thine,
That have profaned their scarlet ornaments
And seal'd false bonds of love as oft as mine,
Robb'd others' beds' revenues of their rents.

Be it lawful I love thee, as thou lov'st those
Whom thine eyes woo as mine importune thee ;
Root pity in thy heart, that when it grows
Thy pity may deserve to pitied be.

   If thou dost seek to have what thou dost hide,
   By self-example mayst thou be denied !

A PICTURE

LO ! as a careful housewife runs to catch
     One of her feather'd creatures broke away,
Sets down her babe and makes all swift despatch
In pursuit of the thing she would have stay,

Whilst her neglected child holds her in chase,
Cries to catch her whose busy care is bent
To follow that which flies before her face,
Not prizing her poor infant's discontent ;

So runn'st thou after that which flies from thee,
Whilst I, thy babe, chase thee afar behind ;
But if thou catch thy hope, turn back to me,
And play the mother's part, kiss me, be kind :

    So will I pray that thou mayst have thy ' Will,'
    If thou turn back, and my loud crying still.

EROS AND ANTEROS

TWO loves I have of comfort and despair,
 Which like two spirits do suggest me still :
The better angel is a man right fair,
The worser spirit a woman colour'd ill.

To win me soon to hell, my female evil
Tempteth my better angel from my side,
And would corrupt my saint to be a devil,
Wooing his purity with her foul pride.

And whether that my angel be turn'd fiend
Suspect I may, yet not directly tell ;
But being both from me, both to each friend,
I guess one angel in another's hell :

 Yet this shall I ne'er know, but live in doubt,
 Till my bad angel fire my good one out.

ALL'S WELL THAT ENDS WELL

THOSE lips that Love's own hand did make
    Breathed forth the sound that said 'I hate'
To me that languish'd for her sake ;
But when she saw my woeful state,

Straight in her heart did mercy come,
Chiding that tongue that, ever sweet,
Was used in giving gentle doom,
And taught it thus anew to greet ;

'I hate' she alter'd with an end,
That follow'd it as gentle day
Doth follow night, who like a fiend
From heaven to hell is flown away ;

    'I hate' from hate away she threw,
    And saved my life, saying 'not you.'

SOUL AND BODY

POOR soul, the centre of my sinful earth,
   [Foil'd by] these rebel powers that thee array,
Why dost thou pine within and suffer dearth,
Painting thy outward walls so costly gay?

Why so large cost, having so short a lease,
Dost thou upon thy fading mansion spend?
Shall worms, inheritors of this excess,
Eat up thy charge? is this thy body's end?

Then, Soul, live thou upon thy servant's loss,
And let that pine to aggravate thy store;
Buy terms divine in selling hours of dross;
Within be fed, without be rich no more:

  So shalt thou feed on Death, that feeds on men,
  And Death once dead, there's no more dying
     then.

MADNESS OF LOVE

MY love is as a fever, longing still
        For that which longer nurseth the disease,
Feeding on that which doth preserve the ill,
The uncertain sickly appetite to please.

My reason, the physician to my love,
Angry that his prescriptions are not kept,
Hath left me, and I desperate now approve
Desire is death, which physic did except.

Past cure I am, now reason is past care,
And frantic-mad with evermore unrest;
My thoughts and my discourse as madmen's are,
At random from the truth vainly express'd;

    For I have sworn thee fair and thought thee
            bright,
    Who art as black as hell, as dark as night.

PASSION-BLINDNESS

O ME, what eyes hath Love put in my head,
　　Which have no correspondence with true
　　　sight !
Or, if they have, where is my judgment fled,
That censures falsely what they see aright?

If that be fair whereon my false eyes dote,
What means the world to say it is not so?
If it be not, then love doth well denote
Love's ' eye ' is not so true as all men's ' no : '—

How can it ?   O, how can Love's eye be true,
That is so vex'd with watching and with tears ?
No marvel then, though I mistake my view ;
The sun itself sees not till heaven clears.

　O cunning Love ! with tears thou keep'st me
　　blind,
Lest eyes well-seeing thy foul faults should find.

A LAST APPEAL

CANST thou, O cruel! say I love thee not,
    When I against myself with thee partake?
Do I not think on thee, when I forgot
Am of myself, all tyrant, for thy sake?

Who hateth thee that I do call my friend?
On whom frown'st thou that I do fawn upon?
Nay, if thou lour'st on me, do I not spend
Revenge upon myself with present moan?

What merit do I in myself respect,
That is so proud thy service to despise,
When all my best doth worship thy defect,
Commanded by the motion of thine eyes?

But, Love, hate on, for now I know thy mind;
Those that can see thou lov'st, and I am blind.

DE PROFUNDIS

O, FROM what power hast thou this powerful
might
With insufficiency my heart to sway?
To make me give the lie to my true sight,
And swear that brightness doth not grace the day?

Whence hast thou this becoming of things ill,
That in the very refuse of thy deeds
There is such strength and warrantise of skill
That, in my mind, thy worst all best exceeds?

Who taught thee how to make me love thee more
The more I hear and see just cause of hate?
O, though I love what others do abhor,
With others thou shouldst not abhor my state:

If thy unworthiness raised love in me,
More worthy I to be beloved of thee.

VANITAS VANITATUM

IN loving thee thou know'st I am forsworn,
 But thou art twice forsworn, to me love
  swearing,
In act thy bed-vow broke and new faith torn
In vowing new hate after new love bearing.

.But why of two oaths' breach do I accuse thee,
When I break twenty? I am perjured most ;
For all my vows are oaths but to misuse thee,
And all my honest faith in thee is lost,

For I have sworn deep oaths of thy deep kindness,
Oaths of thy love, thy truth,. thy constancy,
And, to enlighten thee, gave eyes to blindness,
Or made them swear against the thing they see ;

 For I have sworn thee fair ; more perjured I,
 To swear against the truth so foul a lie !

YOUTH AND AGE

CRABBÉD Age and Youth cannot live together :
    Youth is full of pleasance, age is full of care ;
Youth like summer morn, age like winter weather ;
Youth like summer brave, age like winter bare.

Youth is full of sport, age's breath is short ;
    Youth is nimble, age is lame ;
Youth is hot and bold, age is weak and cold ;
    Youth is wild, and age is tame.

Age, I do abhor thee ; Youth, I do adore thee ;
    O, my Love, my Love is young !
Age, I do defy thee : O, sweet shepherd, hie thee,
    For methinks thou stay'st too long.

FAIR AND FALSE

FAIR is my Love, but not so fair as fickle ;
    Mild as a dove, but neither true nor trusty ;
Brighter than glass, and yet, as glass is, brittle ;
Softer than wax, and yet, as iron, rusty :
    A lily pale, with damask dye to grace her,
    None fairer, nor none falser to deface her.

Her lips to mine how often hath she join'd,
Between each kiss her oaths of true love swearing !
How many tales to please me hath she coin'd,
Dreading my love, the loss thereof still fearing !
    Yet in the midst of all her pure protestings,
    Her faith, her oaths, her .tears, and all were
        jestings.

She burn'd with love, as straw with fire flameth ;
She burn'd out love, as soon as straw out-burneth ;
She framed the love, and yet she foil'd the framing ;
She bade love last, and yet she fell a-turning.
    Was this a lover, or a lecher whether ?
    Bad in the best, though excellent in neither.

TO-MORROW

LORD, how mine eyes throw gazes to the east !
    My heart doth charge the watch; the morn-
        ing rise
Doth cite each moving sense from idle rest.
Not daring trust the office of mine eyes,
    While Philomela sits and sings, I sit and mark,
    And wish her lays were tunéd like the lark ;

For she doth welcome daylight with her ditty,
And drives away dark dismal-dreaming night :
The night so pack'd, I post unto my pretty ;
Heart hath his hope, and eyes their wishéd sight ;
    Sorrow changed to solace, solace mix'd with
        sorrow ;
    For why, she sigh'd, and bade me come to-
        morrow.

Were I with her, the night would post too soon ;
But now are minutes added to the hours ;
To spite me now, each minute seems a moon ;
Yet not for me, shine sun to succour flowers !
   Pack night, peep day ; good day, of night now
      borrow :
   Short, night, to-night, and length thyself to-
      morrow.

FAREWELL

*G*OOD *night, good rest.*   Ah, neither be my
    share :
She bade good night that kept my rest away ;
And daff'd me to a cabin hang'd with care,
To descant on the doubts of my decay.
   Farewell, quoth she, *and come again to-morrow :*
   Fare well I could not, for I supp'd with sorrow.

Yet at my parting sweetly did she smile,
In scorn or friendship, nill I construe whether :
'T may be, she joyed to jest at my exile,
'T may be, again to make me wander thither :
   Wander, a word for shadows like myself,
   As take the pain, but cannot pluck the pelf.

BEAUTY

BEAUTY is but a vain and doubtful good ;
   A shining gloss that vadeth suddenly ;
A flower that dies when first it 'gins to bud ;
A brittle glass that's broken presently :
   A doubtful good, a gloss, a glass, a flower,
   Lost, vaded, broken, dead within an hour.

And as goods lost are seld or never found,
As vaded gloss no rubbing will refresh,
As flowers dead lie wither'd on the ground,
As broken glass no cement can redress,
   So beauty blemish'd once, 's for ever lost,
   In spite of physic, painting, pain and cost.

AN ELEGY

SWEET Rose, fair Flower, untimely pluck'd, soon
    vaded,
Pluck'd in the bud, and vaded in the spring !
Bright orient pearl, alack, too timely shaded !
Fair creature, kill'd too soon by death's sharp sting !
  Like a green plum that hangs upon a tree,
  And falls, through wind, before the fall should
    be.

I weep for thee, and yet no cause I have ;
For why, thou left'st me nothing in thy will :
And yet thou left'st me more than I did crave ;
For why, I cravéd nothing of thee still :
  —O yes, dear friend, I pardon crave of thee,
  Thy discontent thou didst bequeath to me.

THE PHOENIX AND THE TURTLE

LET the bird of loudest lay,
On the sole Arabian tree,
Herald sad and trumpet be,
To whose sound chaste wings obey.

But thou shrieking harbinger,
Foul precurrer of the fiend,
Augur of the fever's end,
To this troop come thou not near !

From this session interdict
Every fowl of tyrant wing,
Save the eagle, feather'd king :
Keep the obsequy so strict.

Let the priest in surplice white
That defunctive music can,
Be the death-divining swan,
Lest the requiem lack his right.

And thou treble-dated crow,
That thy sable gender makest
With the breath thou giv'st and takest,
'Mongst our mourners shalt thou go.

Here the anthem doth commence :
Love and constancy is dead ;
Phoenix and the turtle fled
In a mutual flame from hence.

So they loved, as love in twain
Had the essence but in one ;
Two distincts, division none :
Number there in love was slain.

Hearts remote, yet not asunder ;
Distance, and no space was seen
'Twixt the turtle and his queen :
But in them it were a wonder.

So between them love did shine,
That the turtle saw his right
Flaming in the phoenix' sight ;
Either was the other's mine.

Property was thus appall'd,
That the self was not the same ;
Single nature's double name
Neither two nor one was call'd.

Reason, in itself confounded,
Saw division grow together,
To themselves yet either neither,
Simple were so well compounded,

That it cried, How true a twain
Seemeth this concordant one !
Love hath reason, reason none,
If what parts can so remain.

Whereupon it made this threne
To the phoenix and the dove
Co-supremes and stars of love,
As chorus to their tragic scene.

THRENOS

Beauty, truth, and rarity,
Grace in all simplicity,
Here enclosed in cinders lie.

Death is now the phoenix' nest ;
And the turtle's loyal breast
To eternity doth rest,

Leaving no posterity :
'Twas not their infirmity,
It was married chastity.

Truth may seem, but cannot be ;
Beauty brag, but 'tis not she ;
Truth and beauty buried be.

To this urn let those repair
That are either true or fair ;
For these dead birds sigh a prayer.

A LOVER'S COMPLAINT

—οἵαν τὰν ὑάκινθον ἐν ὥρεσι ποίμενες ἄνδρες
πόσσι καταστείβοισι, χάμαι δέ τε πόρφυρον ἄντυς—

A LOVER'S COMPLAINT

FROM off a hill whose concave womb re-worded
       A plaintful story from a sistering vale,
My spirits to attend this double voice accorded,
And down I laid to list the sad-tuned tale ;
Ere long espied a fickle maid full pale,
Tearing of papers, breaking rings a-twain,
Storming her world with sorrow's wind and rain.

Upon her head a platted hive of straw,
Which fortified her visage from the sun,
Whereon the thought might think sometime it saw
The carcass of a beauty spent and done :
Time had not scythéd all that youth begun,
Nor youth all quit ; but, spite of heaven's fell rage,
Some beauty peep'd through lattice of sear'd age.

Oft did she heave her napkin to her eyne,
Which on it had conceited characters,
Laundering the silken figures in the brine
That season'd woe had pelleted in tears,
And often reading what contents it bears ;
As often shrieking undistinguish'd woe,
In clamours of all size, both high and low.

Sometimes her levell'd eyes their carriage ride,
As they did battery to the spheres intend ;
Sometimes diverted their poor balls are tied
To the orbéd earth ; sometimes they do extend
Their view right on ; anon their gazes lend
To every place at once, and, nowhere fix'd,
The mind and sight distractedly commix'd.

Her hair, nor loose nor tied in formal plat,
Proclaim'd in her a careless hand of pride :
For some. untuck'd, descended her sheaved hat,
Hanging her pale and pinéd cheek beside ;
Some in her threaden fillet still did bide,
And, true to bondage, would not break from thence,
Though slackly braided in loose negligence.

A' thousand favours from a maund she drew
Of amber, crystal, and of beaded jet,
Which one by one she in a river threw,
Upon whose weeping margent she was set ;
Like usury, applying wet to wet,
Or monarch's hands that let not bounty fall
Where want cries some, but where excess begs all.

Of folded schedules had she many a one,
Which she perused, sigh'd, tore, and gave the flood ;
Crack'd many a ring of posied gold and bone,
Bidding them find their sepulchres in mud ;
Found yet moe letters sadly penn'd in blood,
With sleided silk feat and affectedly
Enswathed, and seal'd to curious secrecy.

These often bathed she in her fluxive eyes,
And often kiss'd, and often 'gan to tear ;
Cried " O false blood, thou register of lies,
What unapprovéd witness dost thou bear !
Ink would have seem'd more black and damnéd
    here ! "
This said, in top of rage the lines she rents,
Big discontent so breaking their contents.

A reverend man that grazed his cattle nigh--
Sometime a blusterer, that the ruffle knew
Of court, of city, and had let go by
The swiftest hours, observéd as they flew—
Towards this afflicted fancy fastly drew,
And, privileged by age, desires to know
In brief the grounds and motives of her woe.

So slides he down upon his grainéd bat,
And comely-distant sits he by her side;
When he again desires her, being sat,
Her grievance with his hearing to divide :
If that from him there may be aught applied
Which may her suffering ecstasy assuage,
'Tis promised in the charity of age.

" Father," she says, " though in me you behold
The injury of many a blasting hour,
Let it not tell yóur judgment I am old ;
Not age, but sorrow, over me hath power :
I might as yet have been a spreading flower,
Fresh to myself, if I had self-applied
Love to myself, and to no love beside.

" But, woe is me ! too early I attended
A youthful suit—it was to gain my grace—
Of one by nature's outwards so commended,
That maidens' eyes stuck over all his face :
Love lack'd a dwelling, and made him her place ;
And when in his fair parts she did abide,
She was new lodged and newly deified.

" His browny locks did hang in crooked curls ;
And every light occasion of the wind
Upon his lips their silken parcels hurls.
What's sweet to do, to do will aptly find :
Each eye that saw him did enchant the mind,
For on his visage was in little drawn
What largeness thinks in Paradise was sawn.

" Small show of man was yet upon his chin ;
His phoenix down began but to appear
Like unshorn velvet on that termless skin
Whose bare out-bragg'd the web it seem'd to wear :
Yet show'd his visage by that cost more dear;
And nice affections wavering stood in doubt
If best were as it was, or best without.

ᐸ

" His qualities were beauteous as his form,
For maiden-tongued he was, and therefore free ;
Yet, if men moved him, was he such a storm
As oft 'twixt May and April is to see,
When winds breathe sweet, unruly though they be.
His rudeness so with his authórized youth
Did livery falseness in a pride of truth.

" Well could he ride, and often men would say
That horse his mettle from his rider takes :
Proud of subjection, noble by the sway,
What rounds, what bounds, what course, what stop
    he makes !
And controversy hence a question takes,
Whether the horse by him became his deed,
Or he his manage by the well-doing steed.

" But quickly on this side the verdict went :
His real habitude gave life and grace
To appertainings and to ornament,
Accomplish'd in himself, not in his case :
All aids, themselves made fairer by their place,
Came for additions ; yet their purposed trim
Pieced not his grace, but were all graced by him.

Q

" So on the tip of his subduing tongue
All kind of arguments and question deep
All replication prompt and reason strong
For his advantage still did wake and sleep :
To make the weeper laugh, the laugher weep,
He had the dialect and different skill,
Catching all passions in his craft of will :

" That he did in the general bosom reign
Of young, of old ; and sexes both enchanted,
To dwell with him in thoughts, or to remain
In personal duty, following where he haunted :
Consents bewitch'd, ere he desire, have granted ;
And dialogued for him what he would say,
Ask'd their own wills, and made their wills obey.

" Many there were that did his picture get,
To serve their eyes, and in it put their mind;
Like fools that in th' imagination set
The goodly objects which abroad they find
Of lands and mansions, theirs in thought assign'd :
And labouring in moe pleasures to bestow them
Than the true gouty landlord which doth owe them:

"So many have, that never touch'd his hand,
Sweetly supposed them mistress of his heart.
—My woeful self that did in freedom stand,
And was my own fee-simple, not in part,
What with his art in youth, and youth in art,
Threw my affections in his charméd power,
Reserved the stalk, and gave him all my flower.

"Yet did I not, as some my equals did,
Demand of him, nor being desired yielded ;
Finding myself in honour so forbid,
With safest distance I mine honour shielded :
Experience for me many bulwarks builded
Of proofs new-bleeding, which remain'd the foil
Of this false jewel, and his amorous spoil.

"But ah ! who ever shunn'd by precedent
The destined ill she must herself assay?
Or forced examples, 'gainst her own content,
To put the by-past perils in her way?
Counsel may stop a while what will not stay ;
For when we rage, advice is often seen
By blunting us to make our wits more keen.

" Nor gives it satisfaction to our blood,
That we must curb it upon others' proof ;
To be forbod the sweets that seem so good,
For fear of harms that preach in our behoof.
O Appetite, from Judgement stand aloof !
The one a palate hath that needs will taste,
Though Reason weep, and cry *It is thy last.*

" For further I could say *This man's untrue,*
And knew the patterns of his foul beguiling ;
Heard where his plants in others' orchards grew,
Saw how deceits were gilded in his smiling ;
Knew vows were ever brokers to defiling ;
Thought characters and words merely but art,
And bastards of his foul adulterate heart.

" And long upon these terms I held my city,
Till thus he gan besiege me : *Gentle maid,*
Have of my suffering youth some feeling pity,
And be not of my holy vows afraid:
That's to ye sworn to none was ever said ;
For feasts of love I have been call'd unto,
Till now did ne'er invite, nor never woo.

" *All my offences that abroad you see*
Are errors of the blood, none of the mind;
Love made them not: with acture they may be,
Where neither party is nor true nor kind:
They sought their shame that so their shame did find;
And so much less of shame in me remains,
By how much of me their reproach contains.

" *Among the many that mine eyes have seen,*
Not one whose flame my heart so much as warm'd,
Or my affection put to the smallest teen,
Or any of my leisures ever charm'd:
Harm have I done to them, but ne'er was harm'd;
Kept hearts in liveries, but mine own was free,
And reign'd, commanding in his monarchy.

" *Look here, what tributes wounded fancies sent me*
Of paléd pearls and rubies red as blood;
Figuring that they their passions likewise lent me
Of grief and blushes, aptly understood
In bloodless white and the encrimson'd mood;
Effects of terror and dear modesty,
Encamp'd in hearts, but fighting outwardly.

" *And, lo, behold these talents of their hair,*
With twisted metal amorously impleach'd,
I have received from many a several fair,
Their kind acceptance weepingly beseech'd,
With the annexions of fair gems enrich'd,
And deep-brain'd sonnets that did amplify
Each stone's dear nature, worth, and quality.

" *The diamond,—why, 'twas beautiful and hard,*
Whereto his invised properties did tend;
The deep-green emerald, in whose fresh regard
Weak sights their sickly radiance do amend;
The heaven-hued sapphire and the opal blend
With objects manifold: each several stone,
With wit well blazon'd, smiled or made some moan.

" *Lo, all these trophies of affections hot,*
Of pensived and subdued desires the tender,
Nature hath charged me that I hoard them not,
But yield them up where I myself must render,
That is, to you, my origin and ender;
For these, of force, must your oblations be,
Since I their altar, you enpatron me.

" *O, then, advance of yours that phraseless hand,*
Whose white weighs down the airy scale of praise ;
Take all these similes to your own command,
Hallow'd with sighs that burning lungs did raise ;
What me your minister, for you obeys,
Works under you : and to your audit comes
Their distract parcels in combinéd sums.

" *Lo, this device was sent me from a nun,*
Or sister sanctified, of holiest note ;
Which late her noble suit in court did shun,
Whose rarest havings made the blossoms dote ;
For she was sought by spirits of richest coat,
But kept cold distance, and did thence remove,
To spend her living in eternal love.

" *But, O my sweet, what labour is 't to leave*
The thing we have not, mastering what not strives,
Playing the place which did no form receive,
Playing patient sports in unconstrainéd gyves ?
She that her fame so to herself contrives,
The scars of battle 'scapeth by the flight,
And makes her absence valiant, not her might.

" O, pardon me, in that my boast is true :
The accident which brought me to her eye
Upon the moment did her force subdue,
And now she would the cagéd cloister fly :
Religious love put out Religion's eye :
Not to be tempted, would she be immured ;
And now, to tempt, all liberty procured.

" How mighty then you are, O hear me tell !
The broken bosoms that to me belong
Have emptied all their fountains in my well,
And mine I pour your ocean all among :
I strong o'er them, and you o'er me being strong,
Must for your victory us all congest,
As compound love to physic your cold breast.

" My parts had power to charm a sacred nun,
Who, disciplined, ay, dieted in grace,
Believed her eyes when they to assail begun,
All vows and consecrations giving place :
O most potential love ! vow, bond, nor space,
In thee hath neither sting, knot, nor confine,
For thou art all, and all things else are thine.

" When thou impressest, what are precepts worth
Of stale example ?   When thou wilt inflame,
How coldly those impediments stand forth
Of wealth, of filial fear, law, kindred, fame!
Love's arms are peace, 'gainst rule, 'gainst sense,
*   'gainst shame,*
And sweetens, in the suffering pangs it bears,
The aloes of all forces, shocks, and fears.

" Now all these hearts that do on mine depend,
Feeling it break, with bleeding groans they pine;
And supplicant their sighs to you extend,
To leave the battery that you make 'gainst mine,
Lending soft audience to my sweet design,
And credent soul to that strong-bonded oath
That shall prefer and undertake my troth.

"This said, his watery eyes he did dismount,
Whose sights till then were levell'd on my face ;
Each cheek a river running from a fount
With brinish current downward flow'd apace :
O, how the channel to the stream gave grace !
Who glazed with crystal gate the glowing roses
That flame through water which their hue encloses.

" O father, what a hell of witchcraft lies
In the small orb of one particular tear !
But with the inundation of the eyes
What rocky heart to water will not wear ?
What breast so cold that is not warméd here ?
O cleft effect ! cold modesty, hot wrath,
Both fire from hence and chill extincture hath.

" For, lo, his passion, but an art of craft,
Even there resolved my reason into tears ;
There my white stole of chastity I daff'd,
Shook off my sober guards and civil fears ;
Appear to him, as he to me appears,
All melting ; though our drops this difference bore,
His poison'd me, and mine did him restore.

" In him a plenitude of subtle matter,
Applied to cautels, all strange forms receives,
Of burning blushes, or of weeping water,
Or swooning paleness ; and he takes and leaves,
In either's aptness, as it best deceives,
To blush at speeches rank, to weep at woes,
Or to turn white and swoon at tragic shows :

" That not a heart which in his level came
Could 'scape the hail of his all-hurting aim,
Showing fair nature is both kind and tame ;
And, veil'd in them, did win whom he would maim:
Against the thing he sought he would exclaim ;
When he most burn'd in heart-wish'd luxury,
He preach'd pure maid, and praised cold chastity.

" Thus merely with the garment of a Grace
The naked and concealéd fiend he cover'd ;
That th' unexperient gave the tempter place,
Which like a cherubin above them hover'd.
Who, young and simple, would not be so lover'd ?
Ay me ! I fell ; and yet do question make
What I should do again for such a sake.

"O that infected moisture of his eye,
O that false fire which in his cheek so glow'd,
O that forced thunder from his heart did fly,
O that sad breath his spongy lungs bestow'd,
O all that borrow'd motion, seeming owed,
Would yet again betray the fore-betray'd,
And new pervert a reconciléd maid ! "

THE END

NOTES

The object of this collection is to bring the purely lyrical works of Shakespeare, and the lyrical only, within a portable volume. The *Venus* and the *Lucrece*, which in modern times have generally accompanied the Sonnets, (as belonging rather to the class Lyrical-narrative, than Lyric pure), are hence omitted, together with a very few sonnets connected closely in subject with the *Venus*, and marked, like it, by a warmth of colouring unsuited for the larger audience—compared with that before the Elizabethan Muses—which poetry now addresses.

The Songs have been arranged under classes : as when grouped thus, the minor lyrics acquire more value, and the series presents a less fragmentary character. Songs too closely involved in the action of the play for intelligible separation from it, and some of doubtful authorship, are not included. In the Sonnets the original order has been preserved. The text is that of the "Globe" edition of 1864. The principle of that edition is a sparing introduction of the most plausible emendations of the most obviously corrupt passages. Except, however, perhaps, in the *Lover's Complaint*, the original texts of the lyrical poetry do not seem so faulty as those of the dramatic. Most of the notes are simply glossarial. For some of the exegetical, the reader is indebted to the kindness of Mr. W. G. Clark.

Pleasure is the object of poetry : and the best fulfilment of its task is the greatest pleasure of the greatest number. ⱽ But pleasure demands intelligibility ; and, in the hope of aiding it, titles have been added to the poems. The editor was here encouraged by the counsel of a friend, distinguished for refinement in poetical criticism ; he has tried to make his titles explanatory to the lovers of poetry, either by way of hint or of more direct statement ; he submits this intrusion upon Shakespeare to their good nature.

There are very few men whose greatness is so conspicuous and imperial, that their writings have obtained a prescriptive right to appear, century after century, without the formality or impertinence of introduction by other hands. Homer, Virgil, Dante, Milton, and Shakespeare are monumental. They move through the ages in a long triumph; and even a Preface cannot presume to go before them. But every book should carry its own history with it, and, so far as possible, its own explanation. A few remarks upon the style and character of the preceding poems are therefore added here, as an *Envoy* to the reader.

F. T. PALGRAVE

Nov. 1865

SONGS FROM THE PLAYS

1   *And Phoebus, &c.*: the sun begins to drink the dew in the flower-cups.
7   *she doth owe*: doth own.
10 *youth and kind*: youth and nature.
16 *On a day*: The version of this song in the *Passionate Pilgrim* reads *gan* for *can*, l. 6, and *Wish'd* for *Wish*, l. 8.
18 *foison*: abundance.
20 *cypres*: crape.
23 *Consign to thee*: become confederates and partakers with thee.
25 *whist*: quiet.
28 *the triple Hecate*: used here for Diana; the moon.
30 *takes his gait*: his way.
33 *pugging tooth*: thieving appetite.
34 *hent the stile*: take it.
36 *toys for your head*: caps.
44 *keel*: generally explained, skim. May it not be, *cool?* Compare *leese* for *lose*.

THE SONNETS

Only three or four generations of fairly long-lived men lie between us and Shakespeare ; literature in his own time had reached a high development ; his grandeur and sweetness were freely recognised ; within seventy years of his death his biography was attempted ; yet we know little more of Shakespeare himself than we do of Homer. Like several of the greatest men,—Lucretius, Virgil, Tacitus, Dante,—a mystery never to be dispelled hangs over his life. He has entered into the cloud. With a natural and an honourable diligence, other men have given their lives to the investigation of his, and many external circumstances, mostly of a minor order, have been thus collected : yet of "the man Shakespeare," in Mr. Hallam's words, we know nothing. Something which seems more than human in immensity of range and calmness of insight moves before us in the Plays; but, from the nature of dramatic writing, the author's personality is inevitably veiled; no letter, no saying of his, or description by any intimate friend, has been preserved : and even when we turn to the *Sonnets*, though each is an autobiographical confession, we find ourselves equally foiled. These revelations of the poet's innermost nature appear to teach us less of the man than the tone of mind which we trace, or seem to trace, in *Measure for Measure*, *Hamlet*, and the *Tempest*: the strange imagery of passion which passes over the magic mirror has no tangible existence before or behind it : — the great artist, like Nature herself, is still latent in his works ; diffused through his own creation.

The *Sonnets*, with the *Lover's Complaint*, were published in 1609 by Thomas Thorpe, an eminent bookseller of that day. Their comparative freedom from typographical misreadings is the single point whence it might be conjectured that Shakespeare was in any way connected with the publication. There it no distinct evidence when he wrote them : a brief reference to certain sonnets of his in the *Palladis Tamia* of Meres (1598), is united by no link with these, and may rather point to the sonnets upon the Venus and Adonis legend. Nor does the dedication (reprinted on page 56) throw any light upon the history of the work. Read as it has generally been, it implies that *Thorpe wishes happiness and fame to Mr. W. H., the only object*, or *author*, or *procurer*, *of the following Sonnets.* Read according to another conjecture, it is *Mr. W. H. who wishes happiness to the only object*, or *author* or *procurer*, of the Sonnets : *—The well-wishing adventurer* being, in this case, referred to Thorpe's interest in the work as publisher. Of the six interpretations thus possible, the first alone has afforded any reasonable clue : Thorpe being understood by it to dedicate the Sonnets to *the only object of them, Mr. W. H.* Disregarding the *only*, it has been supposed that the male friend, who is certainly addressed in most of these poems, above Shakespeare in position, and younger in age, was William Herbert, third of that family who held the Earldom of Pembroke. If we allow that the other interpretation should yield to the one which thus dedicates the Sonnets to their *object*, the plausible reasons which give that honour to Herbert are, however, open to the difficulty that, as he became Earl in 1601, and Knight of the Garter in 1603, a publisher would not probably address him as Mr. Herbert in 1609 :—nor is it credible that the whole series could have been occasioned by or with any verisimilitude ascribed to one *only* object. No other known, or really plausible name but Herbert's has been suggested. And if we surrender this interpretation, the remaining five throw no light whatever upon the poems. It would be useless to know that Mr. W. H. procured them, or that he wished well to their object, author, or procurer : that he was the author himself is of course inadmissible.

Turning then to the Sonnets themselves, they obviously present a certain sequence or story, which has been wrought out by the ingenuity of Mr. A. Brown (1838) into six " poems," or definite divisions. The Friend is addressed in five of these (pages 57 to 181) ; the Mistress in the last (pages 182 to 206). It should be observed that Mr. Brown has established these divisions to his own satisfaction without deviating from Thorpe's arrangement, which is of the same uncertain authenticity as the other circumstances of the publication. But, allowing that a sequence is obvious, the real obscurity of the *Sonnets* still remains. Like other poems, they are certainly intended to explain their own meaning : nor can the general intention of this be doubtful to any sane mind. It is here, however, that the true perplexity lies. The external facts, could we reach them, are of a very minor importance. A poet's story differs from a narrative in being in itself a creation. It brings its own facts with it. What we have to ask is not the true life of Laura, but how far Petrarch has truly drawn the life of love. So with the *Sonnets.* Their dates, objects, and circumstances of publication belong only to the prose of the matter. Their history must be looked for within. And, when we study this, we can hardly understand, we cannot enter into the strange series of feelings which they paint; we cannot understand how our great and gentle Shakespeare could have submitted himself to such passions ; we have hardly courage to think that he really endured them. Yet reality appears stamped on the *Sonnets*, not less forcibly than the mythical character upon the autobiography of Dante's early days. It would seem as if he who had formed or fathomed the hearts of the beings whom he called into life with a power beyond that of all other men, had intended here to reveal to us the depths of his own, in a drama more tragic than the madness of *Lear*, or the agonies of *Othello*. But such an exhibition differs much in its effect on the mind from the tragedy of the stage. " There is a weakness and folly in all excessive and misplaced affection," says Mr. Hallam, " which is not redeemed by the touches of nobler sentiments that abound in this long series of

R

sonnets. It is impossible not to wish that Shakespeare had never written them." Such excess, however, as it must appear in the light of common day, is perhaps rarely wanting among the gifts of great genius. The poet's nature differs in degree so much from other men's, that we might almost speak of it as a difference in kind. This, in the sublime language of the *Phaedrus*, is that "possession and ecstasy with which the Muses seize on a plastic and pure soul, awakening it and hurrying it forth like a Bacchanal in the ways of song." A sensitiveness unexperienced by lesser men exalts every feeling to a range beyond ordinary sympathies. Friendship blazes into passion. The furnace of love is seven times heated. An imperious instinct demands that Beauty and the songs in which Beauty is celebrated shall, somehow, spite of human faults and faithlessness, and the grave itself, secure the "eternity promised by our ever-living poet." There is a kind of divine madness, as Plato again called it, in all this: the contrasting merits of moderation and sobriety will present themselves to the reader : he may marvel at the idolatry which the author of *Hamlet* and the *Tempest* wastes, or seems to waste, on an unworthy object : he may be inclined to whisper an

invenies alium, si te hic fastidit, Alexin !

—Yet there is, after all, nothing more remarkable or fascinating in English poetry than these personal revelations of the mind of our greatest poet. We read them again and again, and find each time some new proof of his almost superhuman insight into human nature ; of his unrivalled mastery over all the tones of love. We cannot bring ourselves "to wish that Shakespeare had never

written them," or that the world should have wanted perhaps the most powerful and certainly the most singular
utterances of passion which Poetry has yet supplied.
But there is pleasure also in the belief, that this phase of
feeling was transient, and that the sanity which, not less
than ecstasy, is an especial attribute of the great poet,
returned to the Shakespeare whom, with Jonson, we
"love and honour, on this side idolatry, as much as
any."

The style of the *Sonnets* is condensed and metaphorical; those legal terms which have been noticed as
of frequent occurrence in Shakespeare are here profusely
scattered, and often with an unsatisfactory effect. Like
the Plays, the *Sonnets* share also in that artificiality of
language which was inevitable to the authors of the
" Elizabethan " period, from the circumstances that when
English was first steadily employed on literature, it was not
(what one naturally inclines to think it, from the freshness
of those early flowers) a young language; and that its
literary cultivation was affected, not, like the Hellenic, by a
spontaneous movement of the nation at large, but by writers
educated under diverse and often exotic influences.
Shakespeare is, in this sense, everywhere the child of his
age; but nowhere, it must be confessed, more so than in
the Sonnets. " The obscurity is often such," Mr. Hallam
observes, "as only conjecture can penetrate." And
even conjecture, though learned and ingenious, has been
sometimes at fault. The poetical form adopted is here,
however, partly responsible. Although, in place of the
strict and elegantly involved sonnet structure, he has
adopted the freer but less perfect system of quatrains with
a closing couplet, that ingenious and subtle artificiality of

idea which the Provençal or Italian poets strove to realize within the compass of these fourteen-line lyrics is deeply marked upon Shakespeare's " Book of Love."

The *Passionate Pilgrim*, a small collection published by a speculative bookmaker in 1599, contains a few poems ascribable with certainty to Shakespeare: a very few which are dubious : and several either demonstrably not his, or bearing internal signs of other authorship. The latter have been here omitted. The two former classes fill pages 207 to 214. That strange, but strongly Shakespearian piece of fantasy-painting, the *Phoenix and the. Turtle*, appeared in Chester's *Love's Martyr* (1601), with other poems upon the same subject. It was probably suggested in some degree by the Italian allegory of *Torquato Celiano*, translated by Chester himself.

PAGE

57 *content*: happiness, *Or else this glutton be, &c.* : Or you will commit the excess of consuming what is due to the world by your death and your unmarried life.

58 *sum my count*: complete my account.

59 *unear'd*: untilled. *Fond*: foolish.

61 *lovely gaze*: object of gazing. *Will . . that unfair*: will render that unlovely. *Leese*: lose.

64 *who confounds*: who confoundest: a various form, suggested by euphony ; found especially in verbs ending in *d* or *t*.

65 *makeless*: mateless.

67 *convertest*: changest. *E* before *r* was commonly pronounced *ar*.

70 *oft predict*: frequent prediction. *Store*: here used for *children*.

71 *conceit*: fancy, idea.

72 *pupil pen*: pen of a learner. *Fair*: beauty.

74 *that fair thou owest*: that beauty thou ownest.

75 *So is it not, &c.* : I am not like that poet who exaggerates in praise of a painted beauty, coupling her with all other beauty in earth or heaven. *Rondure*: circle, horizon.

77 *expiate*: end.

79 *stell'd*: probably *set* or *fixed*. *Table*: panel for a picture.

83 *twire*: peep, twinkle.

85 *And with old woes, &c.* · compare the Greek, καινοῖς παλαιὰ δακρύοις στένειν κακά. *Expense*: loss.

PAGE

86 *obsequious tear*: beside the obvious sense, is here used with reference to the *obsequies* of the dead.

88 *region cloud*: cloud overspreading the part of the landscape in view. *Stain*: used as a verb neuter; *be darkened*. So possibly Shelley 'Bare woods, whose branches stain.'

90 *Authorising thy trespass, &c.*: giving a precedent for thy fault by comparing it with mine.

91 *one respect*: one thing we look too. *Separable spite*: a fate that separates us.

92 *I, made lame by fortune's dearest spite*: extremest.—The lameness spoken of here, and on page 144, must be a metaphorical phrase, or an allusion to some passing infirmity. The defect would otherwise have hardly missed notice from those who described Shakespeare's own stage appearances. *Entitled in thy parts*: ennobled in thy genius.

96 *my seat*: property.

98 *unrespected*: unregarded.

101 *quest*: inquest; jury.

104 *advised respects*: considerations formed by reflection.

107 *For blunting*: for fear of blunting. *Carcanet*: necklace.

109 *canker-blooms*: the commentators say, *dog-roses*.

115 *Nativity, once in the main of light, &c.*: when a star has risen and entered on the full stream of light. *Crooked eclipse*: probably as coming athwart the sun's apparent course.

120 *Time's chest*: in which he puts treasures out of sight.

119—121. These three sonnets form one poem of marvellous power, insight, and beauty.

122 *lace*: decorate. *Dead seeing*: lifeless resemblance.

125 *suspect*: suspicion.

129 *The coward conquest, &c.*: must allude to anatomical dissection, then recently revived in Europe by Vesalius, Fallopius, Paré, and others.

131 *a noted weed*: familiar dress.

135 It is entirely unknown to what contemporary poet Shakespeare here alludes. See also page 141, where the same poet appears to be charged with magical practices, like those of Dr. Dee. To commentators interested in discovering the groundwork of the *Sonnets*, these hints should supply a clue.—The superstitions which so strongly mark Europe during the sixteenth century were, in part, the unscientific expression of that advance in the human mind which created physical science again (dormant since the Roman conquest of the Greek states), by the labours of Copernicus, Tyco Brahe, Galileo, Bacon, Gilbert, and many more.

138 *slept in your report*: refrained from writing about you.

139 *example*: used as a verb active; give examples. So *shall fame*.

140 *Reserve*: preserve.

142 *upon misprision growing*: apparently, granted in error.

143 *set one light*: value lightly.

PAGE

144 *To set a form, &c.* : by defining the change you desire.
152 *time removed* : time when I was absent.
153 *heavy Saturn* : the gloomy side of Nature; or, the saturnine spirit in life.
154 *The lily, &c.* : I charged it with stealing the whiteness of thy hand.—This Sonnet contains fifteen lines; a variation which suggests how the sonnet form might be judiciously expanded.
162 *a confined doom* : a defined doom. *And Peace proclaims, &c.* : The peace completed early in 1609, which ended the war between Spain and the United Provinces, might answer to the tone of this Sonnet. Mr. Massey dates it at the accession of James I : and argues that the *eclipse* of the *mortal moon* refers to the death of Elizabeth *Subscribes* : submits.
165 *a motley* : a fool. *Blenches* : deviations.
166 *eisel* : vinegar.
167 *charges* has been here conjectured for *changes*.
168 *latch* : catch. *Favour* : face.
171 *It is the star, &c.* : apparently, whose stellar influence is unknown, although his angular altitude has been determined.
173 *eager* : sour.
174 *limbecks* : alembics used in distillation. *Applying fears, &c.* : setting fears against hopes.
176 *bevel* : aslant ; biassed like a bowl.
177 *retention* : the album, meant to retain memoranda.
179 *state* : seems to mean, *circumstance*. *The fools of time, &c.* : apparently, the plotters and political martyrs of the age.
180 *mutual render* : give-and-take. This sonnet appears directed against some one who had charged him with superficial love.
181 *quietus* : acquittance.
182 *false esteem* : false pretensions.
183 *jacks* : keys.
185 *compare* : comparison.
189 *statute* : security. *A friend came, &c.* : who became.
190 *Let no unkind, &c.* : let no unkindness, no fairspoken rivals destroy me.
192 *a several plot* : a plot severed for a time from a common.
193 This sonnet was published in the *Passionate Pilgrim* of 1599. Shakespeare was then in his thirty-fifth year.
201 [*Foil'd by*] : another conjecture is *Fool'd by*. The original text carelessly repeats *My sinful earth* from the line above.
202 *I desperate now approve, &c.* : I now discover that desire which reason rejected, is death.
203 *censures* : judges.
208 *None fairer, &c.* : She is surpassed by no woman in fairness and in falseness.
214 *shrieking harbinger* : possibly, the screech-owl.
215 *defunctive music* : funeral music. *That thy sable, &c.* : appears an allusion to some legendary fancy
216 *But in them* : except in them. *Property was, &c.* : natural law was astonished to see a thing not identical with itself :—

PAGE

one of the many ingenious plays of fancy,—a fancy almost
arithmetical at times,—in which Shakespeare's subtlety of
mind has indulged itself in this poem. *Property* seems here
used in the logical sense.

227 *Threnos*: dirge.

A LOVER'S COMPLAINT

The form of this poem has some resemblance to the
shorter pieces by or ascribed to Chaucer, such as the
Complaint of the Black Knight: but in its power and
concentration it is probably alone in our language as a
Lyrical Elegy. Under those limitations in regard to
style which have been already noticed, it is such a song as
might have come from the old Aeolian or Ionic poets,
Simonides, or Sappho, or Erinna. Passion as a law to
itself, all for love, and this world well lost, if not the
next also, were never painted with a more sad and
musical intensity.

PAGE

220 *Storming her world:* filling herself and what was around her
with storm. *Napkin:* handkerchief. *Conceited characters:*
fanciful embroideries. *Pelleted:* formed into drops.

221 *their carriage ride:* move themselves. *A careless hand, &c.:*
a hand careless of appearance *Maund:* market-basket with
two lids.

222 *schedules:* billets-doux. *Posied:* bearing mottoes. *With
sleided silk feat* . . . *enswathed:* neatly tied round with floss
silk. *Fancy:* lady-love. *Fastly:* near.

223 *grainéd bat:* rough (?) stick. *Let it not tell, &c.:* observe
this touch of nature!

224 *Sawn:* doubtful whether *sown* or *seen*. *Phoenix down:*
seems to mean either *immortally young*, or *celestially beautiful*. *Bare:* bareness.

225 *became:* graced. *Manage:* skill in riding. *Their purposed
trim, &c.:* artificial accomplishments added nothing to his
grace.

229 *teen:* sorrowful longing; desiderium; sehnsucht. *Talents:*
precious gifts. *Impleach'd:* intertwisted.

PAGE

230   *invised*: a word said to occur only here; either *visible in it*, or *invisible*. *Phraseless*: indescribable. *What me*, &c.: all of mine is your servant, and unites in offering itself to you.

231   *Whose rarest havings*, &c.: whose scantiest favours made youth dote on her. *Playing the place*, &c.: this passage, and *Love's arms are peace*, &c., p. 232, appear hopelessly corrupt.

233   *congest*: combine.

234   *In him a plenitude*, &c.: his abundant subtlety, used for cunning designs.

235   *seeming owed*: apparently his own.

INDEX OF FIRST LINES

www.ingramcontent.com/pod-product-compliance
Lightning Source LLC
Chambersburg PA
CBHW020354030726
47496CB00007B/2135